CENTRAL   c. 1

Koningsberger. Hans.
    Death of a schoolboy ₁by₁ Hans Koning. New York.
Harcourt Brace Jovanovich ₁1974₁
        p.   cm.
    ''A Helen and Kurt Wolff book.''

        1. Princip. Gavrilo. 1894–1918—Fiction.   I.
Title.

PZ4.K83DePS3561.046   813'.5'4   73-18324
Information Design   MARC-CIP

Death of a Schoolboy

Hans Koning

Death of a Schoolboy

A Helen and Kurt Wolff Book

Harcourt Brace Jovanovich, Inc.

New York

About this book

This is a novel, not a documentary account. It is a novel
about history, but I am in no need to claim a special
category for it. The truth of this novel is the truth of its
subject, Gavre Princip; or so I hope.

I have not tried to modernize what happened to him.
It may depress some people, and cheer up others,
but there were indeed freedom marches of schoolboys
as far back as 1913, and they were called just that.

The names in my book are mostly real names.
I have preserved their word image rather than tried to
transcribe them phonetically, for they originate in a
language (Serbo-Croat) with the same alphabet as English.
In that language, though, even letters without accents
are pronounced totally differently from what we would expect.
Thus I have felt free to omit the odd apostrophes and
commas that float over some of them and that don't mean
anything without explanation. I did not want to create
an aura of foreignness with them. My story is not
taking place in a far country.

Printed in the United States of America

Library of Congress Cataloging in Publication Data

Koningsberger, Hans.
     Death of a schoolboy.

     "A Helen and Kurt Wolff book."
     1.   Princip, Gavrilo, 1894–1918—Fiction.   I.   Title.
PZ4.K83De   [PS3561.046]   813'.5'4   73–18324
ISBN 0–15–124155–4
First edition

B C D E

Death of a Schoolboy

Death of a Schoolboy

1

Shackled to a wall, I am telling a story in my mind. Perhaps I should say, reliving my adventure. Reliving my life. None of these words sounds quite right, but I try them out. It's crucial for me not to fall into any traps of turning what happened into a personal drama. If I did, I would be miserable and alone. And I am neither.

When the last light in the corridor is about to go, when I can just distinguish the cross of the two bars in the little half-circle window of my cell door against the grayness behind it, the guard comes in and unlocks my chain from its ring in the stone. Then I can get over to my bunk and lie down for the night. He never says a word to me. He isn't allowed to.

I put the chain under the blanket with me. Its coldness against my body jolts me, but that passes. I used to keep it outside my cover, but discovered that it worked like a drain that way, drawing off my body's warmth and leaving me petrified by dawn. So now I sleep embracing my chain. But the smell, the taste almost, of the rust and the iron is overwhelming. I cannot get used to it. It makes me retch every morning before the tin of barley coffee and the bread help me right myself. Before the guard hands these to me, he fixes my chain back in the ring. I can stand then, or sit on the floor.

Then, slowly, it gets light outside my cell, and the long, the endless day begins. Time, hesitantly, starts to move through my head.

2

My life seems to have followed a circle, from Sarajevo to Belgrade, and then back from Belgrade to Sarajevo to complete it. If I keep that in mind, things will be clearer.

On a sculptured door in the monastery in Belgrade where we used to scrounge free meals, I have seen the emblem of two snakes biting each other's tails. The circle of fate. I'd like to believe in those things, they are comforting. But I don't, of course.

It was in the fall of 1913, only a couple of years ago, that we organized that freedom march from Sarajevo high school to the town hall. "We" being fifth graders, Bosnians, that is to say, Serbians. Subjects of the Austrian Empire which had occupied our country and then annexed it.

But we weren't thinking in soldier's or politician's language. I am not an Austrian in reverse, and with "Austrian" I think of a world-wide species who have a cog missing in their emotional machines, as if they were on a lower level of evolution. It just happened that where I was born, Bosnia, that species, no matter where from, were Austrian by profession. In Ireland, they were English, and so on.

When we set out on that march, and were expelled for it, we weren't just hoping that one day there'd be Serbian faces looking at us over those policemen's collars. Our ideas were vaguer and wilder, more human. We rarely talked about them to outsiders, though. Let them think what they want to.

After I was expelled, I went back home, to my father's farm in the Grahovo Valley, that is.

I had no choice. My older brother had been paying for my school; when he learned what had happened, he said that was the end of my school days. He was a dealer in wood, and if it hadn't been for him, I'd never have been to school in the first place. I only began when I was nine; my father had me working as a shepherd until then. But he had taught me to read and write.

I lost another year when I switched from the Commercial School to the Latin School. My brother had never forgiven me for that, my stupidly telling him I didn't like commerce and hated the new business section, the pride of our town, with its facts-of-life money men, its contemptuous assumption that we, people like me, weren't different by choice but by failure. Thus, though eighteen, I still had another grade to go.

My brother said no. The last money he gave me was for a ticket to Bugojno, which is as near as the railway gets to my home. There was no point in hanging on in Sarajevo against his will, so I wrapped up my books and spare shirt and underwear and went off.

That was just before New Year's and when I got to Grahovo Valley, the snow was as high as the roof tops. That "valley" is relative; it's very far up into the mountains, and 1913–14 was a bad winter in Bosnia. Not that I minded.

Here is how our house looks: it's all wood, the roof, of wooden shingles, is very steep, to keep the snow off, and sticks out over the porch. The walls are of daubed planks and twigs, whitewashed. As you come in, on the left, the water barrel and a table. On the right, the grain barrel, oats and barley mixed. Next to it, a door leading to the room where our beds stand. The main thing is the hearth in the big room, where there is always a fire, day and night, summer and winter. Its smoke goes out through a vent in the roof, but ours has always drawn well. There are no windows, and the floor is earth, except for the tiles in the fireplace. I was born on that floor, when my mother at the end of a day's hay gathering came home alone and couldn't make it any more to the bed.

It might seem an odd place to come back to, for someone who spent most waking hours studying Latin and Greek and reading books by men and women who worried about all problems of life, except those that take all the work my father and my mother have in them.

But it wasn't. I'm not being theatrical, but to me Grahovo is closer to Troy and Carthage than the well-warmed rooms

5

of our professors. These scrappy mountains have been fought over for the last thousand years, and before that, they were Greek, ruled from Byzantium. Homer isn't about syntax but about despair and courage. We have had five hundred years of Turkish wars and after our last guerrilla battle against them was won, we weren't free but handed over to the nearest Big Power by the other European Powers.

That could not be the end of it. The people always start up again. My father, like everyone here, spends his days in the fields but wakes up only in the evening when he can talk about war and politics. No matter how often they're defeated, they will make war anew. In Latin, that is re-bellare, where the word "rebel" comes from.

I was never looked at with awe as a city scholar by my parents. It fitted in with our history. They thought education was simply the best training for this century and its new kind of battles to come, as once they might have hoped for me to learn archery.

My father didn't berate me over my being expelled. He didn't tell me I should have been grateful and made my peace with the world I was let into. He said, "We must get you to school in Belgrade somehow; we mustn't let the Austrians decide our lives." Because Serbia, of course, and Belgrade, its capital, was where we looked to, a tiny country squeezed between Austrians and Turks, but the only spot where our people were already free—or at least on their own. I wished he would berate me, for he made me ashamed. A kick from an Austrian policeman was a bit pitiful compared with all those ancestors of his silently jailed, hanged, shot.

This man, my father, not any taller than I am (and I'm small), with the same blue eyes, in his red highlander cap and breeches, his leathery hands, wrinkled face; my mother with her tired smile, looking twenty years older than she really was . . . when they kept asking me eagerly about our protests against the authorities, and talked about our past and future hopes, I felt indeed ashamed.

And after that, weariness took hold of me, or more nearly, pity.

Pity for my father and mother and grandfather and on back

through the years, pity for all the bitter integrity of their wasted lives, of their always being on the right side, unknown, undescribed in any newspapers. Poor devil, I thought, as my father was talking, poor devils all of us, imagining that They with a capital T give a damn about whether They're right or wrong in our eyes or in history's eyes. "Go wash, you smell," that's the only reaction his thoughts of a lifetime would have evoked in them.

I remember how, as I thought that, I blushed and looked away, for I had been staring at his hands with their black nails, and was suddenly afraid that he could guess what I was thinking.

What mysterious fuel was he running on? What kept these men and women taking on things as if we had life eternal instead of one second in the century of centuries?

One second. Wasn't that idea enough to paralyze all of us? Or, indeed, to set us all free? What mattered bosses, policemen, armies, prisons, and even the gallows?

What else could we be but free? I am as free as a speck of dirt whirling up from the valley in a stormwind.

3

It was dark in the train compartment and two days of cold tobacco smoke was hanging around us like fog. I was just disentangling myself from my sleeping neighbors when we came to a stop that rained parcels and baskets from the racks all over us.

The winter was nearing its end and I was now on my way to Belgrade to finish school. My freedom-march enthusiasms had gone. Much had happened to me at Grahovo, not outwardly but in my own head.

I don't mean that I had acquired wisdom. More a real, flesh-and-bone awareness of unwisdom, of absurdity. Not of myself, of everything.

The long way from Grahovo had led through Fiume, with

stretches of walking, and riding on peasants' carriages. From Fiume, it was all railroad, and only two different trains all the way to my destination.

The sky over Fiume had been light, and I'd had my one glimpse of the Adriatic Sea, glittering waves brighter blue than I've ever seen anything. Then we turned away from the coast, and the train chugged up through the woods and marshes of Croatia; the sky changed to slate gray and the trees were bare again. After Zagreb, it was night outside, a black vastness with rarely a light blinking. We were back in the harsh snowy inland winter, but the train was so packed with passengers that it kept us warm. The wooden slats of that train bench were carved into my back. You had to stay put at the stops, not to lose your seat.

But this time the conductor ran along the train and cried in various languages, "Border control! Everyone off." We had come to the outer line of the Austrian-Hungarian Empire.

I scrambled out and stood on the platform. There were some electric lamps burning and beyond them it was hard to distinguish much, but in the distance the horizon showed a green strip of dawn light with a thread of orange cloud. A wet wind, wonderful to feel, was blowing in my face. Ahead of us was a wooden barrier and behind it flew the red, blue, and white tricolor of Serbia, the white band picking up the light from the office window behind it. I could see the glimmer of the frontier river, the Sava, under the railway bridge back of the platform.

How easy it is to free yourself; I thought I'd never go back.

"Get in line," an Austrian soldier said to me in German. We shuffled toward the gate. I showed my high school pass, all you needed to get across if you were under age. The school had forgotten to get the passes back from those of us they had expelled. The Austrian border guard made me open my bundle but he didn't look up my name. I walked past the Austrian double-headed eagle and, pretending to cough, managed to spit on it.

I know actions like that are silly, but I felt silly. Not that it isn't a very ugly eagle, in very ugly colors. Contrary to what the Austrians believe of themselves, their aesthetics aren't much. And why do nations always want to be likened to eagles and lions? They pounce on their victims but in a different style; for a new Austrian design I'd suggest a dog, something like a cross between a mastiff and a dachshund.

"And you?" the Serbian on the other side of the barrier asked and looked from my worn-out shoes up to my cardboard collar. "Do you have money?"

"Certainly."

"Let's see it."

I fished out what I had left, two Austrian crowns. I began to laugh and he laughed too.

Then he stopped laughing abruptly to show this was a serious matter. "That'll just buy you one round of beers in Belgrade," he said.

"I haven't come to drink beer," I answered. I didn't think he was going to send me back, but it was better to pile it on a bit. "Money," I said as bitterly and contemptuously as I could, "Is that the first thing you ask of an exiled Serbian brother of yours? Perhaps that Austrian there will pay you thirty pieces of silver if you send me back to him."

He was embarrassed. "Alright, alright," he muttered. "Register with the police, within twenty-four hours," and he pointed to the waiting train.

I got back on. Very soon afterward we pulled into Belgrade Station. For the capital of Serbia lay within walking distance of the Austrian-Hungarian border; what a vulnerable city it was!

Dirty piles of snow and mud were still sticking in the corners, and deep puddles came near to flooding the station square. As I picked my way around them, I felt highly pleased with myself.

The sun was above the roofs now, a pale mountain sun. It was early spring, the third of March to be precise. Tuesday, March 3, 1914.

4

Belgrade looked a happy place that first morning. And it has always kept that quality with me.

It was simply happy then with the sun shining after months of snow and sleet. The streets were already packed with carts and carriages, here and there a motorcar, and throngs of people going to work. There were many soldiers around, and veterans from the two Balkan wars in odds and ends of uniform and civilian clothing. Few officers—it was too early for them.

I tramped all across the town, through Kalemegdan Park, where the snow was soft and gleaming, the little Turkish streets, and the new commercial district with its banks under their golden lettering. But I didn't feel that antagonism there that the businessmen of Sarajevo always stir up in us. Perhaps because Serbians, even when they're bankers, are still poor. Or perhaps because they go about their activities with a certain grandeur that no Austrian, or Anglo-Saxon, would ever understand. I mean that you can see they'd sell out their whole bank or incorporated company complete with London-trained accountant over a drink if it were a matter of paying off a brother's debt of honor.

I had a destination, the town square of the flower market. Its bars and coffeehouses served as get-togethers for the exiles from Bosnia and from Hercegovina, students like me, or men who had fought as volunteers in the Serbian army against Turkey and were now unable to go back to their villages in the Austrian-Hungarian Empire.

Only one of these cafés had opened when I got there. It was on a corner, and I, and eventually all my friends, always called it the Cornerbar. It became my real home through my Belgrade time. Not that the first morning the owner eyed me very welcomingly. He could see those two lonely coins through my jacket.

I installed myself with a coffee and started my wait. There

were only tradesmen from the market. The students wouldn't show up until later; you could easily pick them out. They looked thinner, paler, and either talked more loudly or whispered, and like no other person, always carried books under their arms. Some few girls were among them from the high schools. The universities had no girls. We believed in that equality, but girls' parents did not.

The first batch of students to come in had no one I knew. They looked me over but went to sit across the room; they couldn't know I wasn't an informer. The place soon got packed. Those with money in their pockets ordered lunch for themselves and one or two friends. The others kept taking imaginary sips out of their empty coffee cups.

It got quiet again. The owner vanished for a nap in his backroom, I was still sitting there, alone, and I was getting pretty miserable. Then, at last, a boy came in whom I knew and knew well, for he had been in that same Sarajevo school march and had been expelled with me. His name was Djula and he was a Moslem. I had heard that he had been admitted at the university of Belgrade and some religious group had given him a stipend.

What a relief to see him. "Gavre, Gavrica," he shouted, "welcome to Serbia, you renegade Austrian. We thought we'd seen the last of you."

"Don't call me Gavrica," I said, "make it Gavroche if you want to do something for my name."

"Who's Gavroche?" Djula asked eagerly, as if he had been wondering about it for a long time. He always reacted that way; it was a very comforting habit. He sat down and looked at me with a happy face.

"He's a Victor Hugo hero. I used to try and make my parents call me that. They never did."

"Good! You wanted to be a hero."

"Yes. No longer."

"I hope you don't mean that," Djula said solemnly. "Great deeds are being—are being discussed here by us."

We looked at each other and started to laugh. Djula pulled out a paper bag. "I'll share my lunch with you," he announced,

"and I've money for coffee for both of us. Are you broke?"
He unwrapped his bread and divided it in two.

"My father paid for my fare to Belgrade, it's a long haul, way around through Fiume. I've come to finish my last year and do the university entrance exam. I must find a job to live on in the meantime."

Djula whistled. "There are no jobs in Belgrade. If you'd ask for someone to sweep out that market there, you'd see twenty students line up, ten war veterans, and a couple of philosophy professors from the University of Zagreb."

"I'll manage," I said. "How do you think we live in Grahovo?"

Djula slapped me on the back. "We'll manage," he said. "We'll take care of you. I already know a place where you can sleep tonight. The town kennel."

He waited for my reaction, but I only shrugged. As I'd passed his test, he reassured me. "We've most of us stayed there at times, warm, clean straw, and there are always empty stalls. They don't lock them. Cabrinovic discovered it. He'll be here later. And you and he can go to the Orthodox monastery for dinner. I can't go there, of course. I don't need to; I get fifty dinar a month. We'll find you a real bed soon enough. The monks feed you people, if you don't go too often, but you have to pay for your meal with talk and talk and talk. They love to philosophize with the students. Are you ready to discuss transubstantiation?"

I shook my head.

"They've soup there every night," Djula said, "thick, solid, soup, they tell me. Beans. Fish. Sometimes even mutton."

"What is transubstantiation exactly?"

"Don't ask me that," Djula said. "Islamic law doesn't treat of those quaint superstitions. Tell me, how does it feel, eh, to be in Serbia, to see your own language on the street signs and on the public buildings and on the uniforms?"

"Good. Much more than good. And natural."

5

It didn't work so well when I wanted to explain to Djula and Cabri, as I call Nedeljiko Cabrinovic, what had happened to me those two snowed-in months spent at home.

I began to tell them that I had horrified myself with a surge of pity for my father, and they interrupted me and said that meant that I had cut myself off and had become a middle classer. No one but a member of the middle class would feel that way. And, Cabri went on, the word "middle class" was a misnomer; you couldn't be in the middle between attackers and victims, exploiters and exploited. The only characteristics that distinguished a middle classer from an upper classer were his hypocrisy and his lack of talent. Cabri was always hard to stop.

I made a face at him and said that if I had indeed cut myself off, it wasn't to join anyone else, and surely not my natural enemies. Up in Grahovo, I said, I'd sort of taken non-hope.

They looked at each other. I had the impression that they thought I'd simply been intimidated by that expulsion business. "Non-hope?" they both repeated.

"Like this," I said, "if you believe that the world is basically reasonable, basically meant to be just, only then do a streetful of students make sense against a big power. But that's faith, mythology—just like our priests give out."

Was I saying that our freedom march hadn't been any different from a church procession, Cabri asked, and he answered himself that that was wicked nonsense. The purpose of one was to wake up people to their real condition, the purpose of the other to lull them into acceptance of it.

How could I tell them, I thought, about what I only half felt myself, my Grahovo realization that it made no sense to try and force reasonableness onto an unreasonable, silent universe? But that I didn't mind, that I didn't need to fool myself? To the contrary, that it was the only way of surviving on this misery earth without going crazy? It would sound pretentious or artificial. It did to me, in daytime. At night, lying awake, I knew it was true.

Djula was staring through the window at the flower market where a few peasant women were still hanging on, trying to sell their last sad bunches of sweet peas and daffodils.

He turned to me. "Yes," he said, "true, without religion there is no point to action, no matter if it's a religion about God or about men or about principles. But the answer to that is, who are we, sitting smug in a bar, to decide there's no point? Grandiose, Gavroche, to accept life in silence. But not so grandiose to accept it for everyone else in silence."

The universe is silent. Our voices don't carry.

" 'Even if I haven't believed in anything for myself, I'll have fought the misery of our time,' " Cabri cited. "Do you know where that's from?"

"Yes. 'Our graves will be the foundation, of a new life without the crimes of today.' I used to—"

I stopped.

Then my weariness from those train nights and deeper weariness from my Grahovo snow philosophies were gone or anyway went into hiding down within me. I felt warm instead, a feeling of love for those two who were taking me so seriously. And just then, at the same moment, we all suddenly shook hands.

Djula went to the back room to pay for the coffees and then we walked out into the heart of town.

We stayed three abreast, even when we pushed through narrow streets where the shopkeepers were now putting their stuff out on the sidewalks, and we kept our hands on each others' shoulders. I looked at the passers-by who were hastily or irritatedly side-stepping us, and thought that I wasn't a man alone in a new town. We were—I didn't know what, but in any case, "we."

6

In Sarajevo, we had been living in an intense atmosphere, my friends and I, and that only partly by choice. We had formed a group at school, but all groupings were strictly forbidden and we were immediately plunged in secrecy—before there was anything to keep secret.

We read about Russian revolutionaries and the followers of Garibaldi and Mazzini in Italy and talked about unity for Serbs and Croats and Moslems, for all South Slavs. We weren't very specific.

We were painfully alone in all this. When Austria annexed Bosnia and Hercegovina in 1908, the local bigwigs actually celebrated a mass of thanksgiving in the Sarajevo cathedral! and when the bishop, or whatever his proper title is, asked the congregation to kneel and pray for the divine blessing on the House of Habsburg, all those hundreds of people knelt—and not in a spirit of Christian forgiveness, you can be sure, but in fear and greed.

The only ones who remained upright in that enormous church were a bunch of high school boys, standing together.

We wrote poetry, or tried to. Most of it was probably terrible, but we believed that poets should be "the soldiers of thought," that sort of idea. I filled a whole notebook but never showed it to anyone.

We studied the German socialists and had an uneasy time with them, admiring them and at the same time feeling that (conceited as it must sound) our world was more complex. Perhaps I can explain by saying that, unlike them, we loved nature too, loved it as much as our fellow men.

We tried hard to show ourselves to be different. For instance, we were pledged not to drink alcohol. Looking back at it now, it was pedantic, but it was based really on the daily spectacle of the workmen of the town boozing with their bosses' blessing. A public drunk would bring an indulgent little smile to the face of a police guard, the same man who'd crack the ribs of a boy painting an anti-Habsburg slogan on a wall.

It was also a reaction against the materialism of our parents, those who were well to do, that is. Materialism, for while they were all very churchy, they were collaborators, sellers-out to the powers that be. And for what? To get fat and old in peace. They worshiped their own bodies, that's what it came down to. That is what made us ascetics.

I had no money for drinking anyway.

A tougher pledge was, no making love, nothing even near it. If you had a girl, it had to be an idealistic friendship.

There was a lot of theorizing behind that, too. Of course, the few girls in or near our group, or sisters of friends, wouldn't have dreamed of love-making or anything like it. They were virgins, as is the tradition in our Greek Orthodox and Catholic families. As for Moslem or Jewish girls, they weren't ever even seen on the street alone. If a girl had shed the church rules and tried to become a real rebel, it would still make no difference to her in *that*. And we, who believed in the brotherhood of a Slav nation and called each other brother and sister, wouldn't have thought of trying to seduce such a girl. Nor could we, as the others in school did, mess around with some poor waitress or kitchen maid who dreamed of getting married.

You couldn't very well speak up about exploitation and class war and do that.

That exhausted the supply of girls, except for the whores. But we were pledged never to go near them either, that also being considered exploitation and degradation of a fellow human being. Moreover, the brothels of Sarajevo had been installed by the government of His Catholic Highness, Emperor Francis Joseph. There had never been anything like them in Bosnia before the Austrians took over. Officially, it had been done for the military, but we never doubted they were a weapon against the people. It would have been easy enough to put them out of bounds to civilians, as so many other places were.

To the contrary, there had been all sorts of underhand propaganda for them, and they had been furnished in a Viennese pseudo-palatial style such as no one in Sarajevo had ever seen: big mirrors on red velvet, gilded chairs, grand pianos. If one kind of curiosity wouldn't help get a hold on the populace, some other kind would. There were three of them, the Red Star, the Blue Star, and the Green Star, plus some crummy ones. At the bottom was a house called The Last Penny, its name over the door in German and in English.

It was a matter of honor to stay away, but those places haunted me.

The last few months before I left, I had a girl friend. On an autumn day, a bunch of us were sitting in the park, talking; I was a bit aside and only half listening. I saw a girl sitting alone on a bench, reading, and her face was so open and eager that I got up to see what book it was. When I saw the title, I began to laugh and without thinking about it, sat down beside her.

"Why do you laugh?" she asked.

I shrugged. She closed the book and looked at its cover. It was called *The Secrets of the Istanbul Palace* and had a picture of a lady in harem pants holding a dagger. Then she laughed, too. "You think I should throw it in the garbage," she stated.

"Not if it's a library book."

That's how we met. Her name was Vukosava, but later that year she began calling herself Sophia, in honor of Sophia Perovskaya, the Russian student who was hanged for her part in the plot to kill Czar Alexander II. By then she had changed a lot from those Istanbul harem days—not because of me, but because she would have anyway. She was a very gentle creature, as was the original Sophia. One day she burst into tears as we passed an old man who had walked into town from heaven knows where, and who was going to sell three wrinkled apples he put on a piece of newspaper in front of him in the road. But she had a sharp mind and will. Different from me, she liked to face people and she loved to argue, to get at the truth, as she said.

I am shy. I usually soon fell silent at those debates where everyone feels a need to hold forth.

She and I read together and we walked along the streets

and roads at the outskirts of town, where you seldom meet anyone except a carrier on a cart creaking by with wood or grain. We never kissed. She was fifteen. During those walks I'd have spells of being overwhelmed by the softness of her presence, by her body that was so fantastically and breathtakingly different from the body of a boy.

And then later when I was alone, that turned into a desperate need to feel such a body, anyone, any girl. Or just see it. I had never seen a naked girl.

I'd walk past The Last Penny, as if to test myself.

Once, in the middle of the afternoon, as I was about to go in to my landlady and pay her the month's rent for my room, I ran out instead with the money in my hand and made for the Blue Star. They didn't look surprised and begged me to make myself comfortable on a sofa. I looked around, at a couple of army officers and a businessman with congested faces, and sleepy Serbian girls in their laps, and walked out again. I went back home, paid my rent, and in my room I took off my clothes and stared at myself until I thought I'd go crazy. I hated my body then; I wanted it to leave me alone. It helped to put your hand on your prick finally to make yourself come, but not really, and not for long. There seemed to be no close connection or even parallel between one thing and the other.

I'd walk along the riverbank with Sophia and we'd buy a cake and share it. We'd go to the Kosovo Cemetery and steal flowers off the graves and put them on the unmarked stone under which Zerajic lies buried. Zerajic was the student who had committed suicide after trying to shoot our murderous governor Varesanin. Most Sarajevo students took their hats or caps off or bowed their heads whenever they passed the spot on the Emperor Bridge where this had happened.

She and I would talk about such things and never about ourselves.

She was a stranger, a mystery, and yet there were flashes of an intimacy between us, deeper than any I'd had with my own family or with old friends. There was an unknown kind of sweetness in that, a whole person, a whole new life just beyond and then just within my touch.

When I had to leave Sarajevo, we both said we'd write often, and we did. We never said anything about waiting for each other, or how long we would be separated. We'd have felt it humiliating and beneath our dignity to talk in such terms.

I had never mentioned her to my friends. Now in Belgrade I was sorry I hadn't; it would have been nice, Cabri and the others asking me about her in a matter-of-fact way.

Looking at Djula and Cabri, it was difficult not to speculate whether they still stuck to our rules here in Belgrade. I tried to imagine Cabri holding a girl in his arms. I wanted to ask, but didn't.

7

The First Belgrade High School accepted me in the senior grade after an exam that was easy. I am never at odds with books. At the school I found Trifko, another friend I had hoped to get back with. His parents sent him a little money, and he had discovered a boardinghouse that charged him only ten dinar a month. We agreed that as soon as I'd have scrounged up some dinars, I'd move in with him. For another five dinar the landlord was going to put up a second bed in his room. I didn't want anyone else to pay that for me.

I didn't mind the kennel; what others had managed to cope with, I could, too.

I went to the place only after dark and left before it was light. During the weeks I slept there, I never saw anyone. After the second night, the dogs didn't keep me awake, and I found a tap where I could wash. It was a good thing when it was over, though. Toward the end, people seemed to shirk away a bit, while dogs, on the other hand, all came up to me.

I never landed a job in Belgrade, though I was ready to do anything. Djula had been right; there were too many stranded men around. I was quite strong then, but I didn't look it. Through a teacher at school, I found a family that hired me to do Latin tutoring for their two children, but at the end of the first week they refused to pay and I quit.

What did I live on? The money Sophia had sent me.

I struggled with that issue for quite a while. I'm a great man for battles of conscience with myself, and after I had lost (or won) this particular one, I felt very suspicious. "An honest man decides against his own interest," had been a favorite quote of mine. Looking back now, I'm not sorry that I did accept the money, but at the time I couldn't have known that. I promised myself to be more severe from then on.

What happened was that one of Sophia's letters, sent to me care of the Belgrade school, had a postal order for fifty dinar in it. It baffled me where she'd have laid hands on so much money. Later, when I kept asking, she wrote that she had pawned the gold cross which she, like most girls, wore. She said in her letter that I must not be offended or sensitive about it. It wasn't for me personally but "for our cause."

The tricky point was that my life was becoming self-centered, and there wasn't that much cause discernible in it.

Certainly, there was always a discussion going in the Corner-bar about the fate of the Slavs under their three foreign oc-cupations, in the German, the Austrian, and the Russian Em-pire. And we were serious; if Serbia had decided to declare war on the lot of them at once, everyone would have volun-teered. But Serbia wasn't going to do that. We talked about a socialist revolution that would overturn the Francis Joseph imperial pyramid from within. But the visible reality of that Empire was the smug prosperity of Vienna and Budapest.

We were chewing on those subjects like students in Paris on a new style in art.

On occasion, a veteran of the Second Balkan War sat with us. His name was Milan. He was older than the rest of us and had won a medal in action against the Bulgarian army. We liked and admired him; he was very modest. It was his theory that we should all train for war, secretly, of course, or the

Serbian authorities would throw us out. He trusted me and once when I visited him, he showed me a wooden box, hidden in his room, full of hand grenades that he had taken home with him from the army. But whom and where would we fight? Did he have a guerrilla war in mind, as of the Spanish against Napoleon? He said he didn't know, but at least we'd be prepared.

"Well, we can say for ourselves that we went into exile," Cabri told me. And he and I went hungry the nights we didn't dare show our faces at the monastery. But what merit was there in all that?

There was friendship among us, even brotherhood, that nearly ruined word . . . the very opposite of my lonely broodings in Grahovo, where I used to make my way through the snow to a pile of firewood on a hill to sit and stare down into the valley.

But at night in that kennel, before falling asleep in the straw bed I had made for myself, thinking over all that had been said during the day, the reality behind those two settings still looked the same. A silent universe, and without echo.

Spring was changing the look of the town. The shores of the Sava and the Danube and the old cracked walls of the citadel were soft green with new grass.

The Cornerbar owner carried chairs and a table out under a tree.

Girls came into the street with their hair falling down freely and no longer wrapped in scarves. You heard music from open windows, piano from the big houses, voices singing from the poor ones.

As soon as the day ended, it was still winter, and the sun set in pools of cold, yellow mist.

It'd be a lie to say we weren't happy then.

Sundays (when the school and the library were closed) I took my books and walked the two miles out of town to Kosutnjak Park, where I sat and read, in an old pavilion full of broken chairs and potted ferns. I used to stay there until it got too dark to see the words, and then I'd run all the way back into town to get warm again. The second or third time, Milan came by with a whole lot of people out on a picnic, and he saw me and made me come along.

We walked through the park and up into the hills, and when a fog started to seep down on us, we lit a fire and sang songs. A girl whose name I never knew came and sat beside me, and took my hand in hers.

Dusk had descended into the streets when we got back.

At each corner people said good-bye, and when we had passed the theater, I found myself alone with her. We walked without a word, her hand on my arm to show me where to go. She stopped me at the gate of a garden full of plum trees; there were two little houses behind them with no light in the windows. She lifted her face up at me, and I could see her eyes in the half-light, and the gleam of her teeth as she suddenly smiled.

I hesitated, and she turned and ran inside.

I walked back toward the center of town, under a deepening sky that quickly filled with stars. Then people and traffic were once more around me, and all at once the new electric street lights flicked on, the sky turned black, and the street and the houses jumped out of their shadows.

Sound carried farther that evening, voices were brighter, there was a special excitement in the air. I had to go to my straw bed hide-out, but didn't mind. There was promise to everything.

In the middle of the night I woke up and stayed awake. A different "I" seemed to spook around in my head. I thought with something like nostalgia of me in Sarajevo, a very serious boy gone forever.

8

The day I was to move in with Trifko on Carigradska Street was the day of the newspaper clipping.

We had got together in the Cornerbar in the early evening.

We were quiet, perhaps because it was still the same restless, strange weather, with a painfully blue sky very high over the city. Some of us were playing billiards and others were flipping through their schoolbooks.

The door had been propped open, and we could smell the abandoned piles of flowers in the market.

I was watching the billiard game and awaiting my turn to play when Cabri came in. Cabri had gotten himself a job just then as a typesetter; he was already a journeyman printer. He now worked every day until seven. His job was at a leftish Liberal daily, but they had nine-hour shifts like the others.

He handed me an envelope. "You may find this interesting," he said in an odd voice.

There was a clipping in it from a Sarajevo newspaper: I recognized the lettering. I looked at the drawing of a musta-chioed gentleman, with underneath a barber advertising his hair-dying skill. Cabri impatiently pulled the paper out of my hand and turned it over.

An item datelined Vienna. "Our beloved Heir to the Throne," it read, "H.I. & R.H. Archduke Francis Ferdinand of Habsburg, will this summer visit Bosnia and Hercegovina. Thus these newly acquired jewels in the Imperial crown are given the opportunity to attest once more to their loyalty to our Government, and to lay to rest the libelous tongues of Serbia doubt-ing the moral unity of. . . ." and on and on. "Army maneuvers of two Army Corps in Bosnia will convince any neighbor of Austria's strength and her determination that Bosnia will never leave the Habsburg Monarchy. These maneuvers will take place on June 26 and 27. Our capital Sarajevo will be honored by the Archducal visit on June 28."

"June 28," Cabri said.

That date, Vidovdan, Saint Vitus Day, is the anniversary of the battle of Kosovo. In that battle, on the 28th of June of the year 1389, the Serbian medieval state was defeated and destroyed by the Turks. Then began a subjugation which ended five hundred years later in Belgrade (in 1867), when the Turkish garrison in the citadel capitulated; and which ended in Sarajevo . . . not ever, for there the Austrian-Hungarians simply took over from the Turks.

It may be far-fetched, in every sense of the word, for a people to have turned this day into a solemn festival, but that's what we had done. Precisely because we had so little history left, this was the one day to cling to—the way the Jews now have to go back two thousand years or more to come to a day of national meaning. Poor people have to make the best of their poor treasure.

I looked at Cabri. He was pale with anger. "Imagine," he said, "this enemy of ours in every way, this man who picked General Varesanin for the pacification of Bosnia, as he called it, this man who'll finally destroy our identity when he gets on that throne . . . this duke" (he spat out the word) "will have the effrontery to ride into Sarajevo with his *Uhlanen* on our June 28."

"Perhaps he'll come by train," someone said. The clipping was now being passed around.

"Damn you. It's no joke," Cabri muttered.

"No."

"Who sent you this?" he was asked.

"I don't know," Cabri answered. "There was no letter, and the address was written on a typewriter."

We looked at the postmark, which said Zenica.

"I don't know anyone in Zenica," Cabri told us.

"It could have been mailed from there to get around the Sarajevo post office censors."

"That makes no sense, since they published the stuff themselves."

"It does seem strange alright that they published it, and so far in advance. Maybe it's all part of a trick. A provocation, to catch protesters."

Several others agreed that it was a phony item, especially planted in the Sarajevo press. We decided to go to the café of the Hotel Royal where they received the *Zeit*, a Viennese paper. Only I and one other student went in, because we could reasonably well read German. We sat there until midnight on one coffee each, scanning through all the copies going back a month and more, and near choking on all the Herren Doktoren and Herren Geheimraete, but we found nothing about this visit.

When we came outside, the others, who'd said they would wait, naturally had vanished. The square lay abandoned. I had to walk halfway across town to my new place, and when I got there, all was dark. Trifko had told me to make sure to get in before nine, and he would then introduce me to the people and get me a key, but I had forgotten all about that.

It seemed a bad idea to start off my stay in that boardinghouse by waking up the landlord. I tried to locate Trifko's window but I wasn't sure of it, and there was nothing at hand to throw anyway.

I stood a while in the silent street, undecided. I had looked forward to sleeping in a real bed. Also, Trifko had my books and stuff in his room. I wondered if I should pull the bell.

I found my thoughts wandering.

I tried to see that famous Kosovo battle as it must have looked, but I couldn't get the participants suitably dressed. We kept appearing in jackets, collars, and ties, while the Turks were mostly in redingotes that flapped in the wind as they pursued us—long cutaways such as I had seen the Sultan wear in a photograph in an illustrated magazine. *Solemn opening of the new brothel on the Grande Rue in Istanbul; H.S.H. Sultan Mohammed VI, seen here graciously welcoming H.R.H. the King of Belgium with the right hand while scratching his crotch with the left.* How tiresome those satraps and dukes and bosses and deans and police commissioners and presidents really were, tiresome and pathetic rather than dangerous; if they could only be taught to get rid of their aggressions in some harmless way, say in daily visits to a brothel or an opium den—

I sat in the doorway of the boardinghouse and dozed with my head against the wall. When the maid came down at dawn to unlock the door, I tiptoed upstairs to Trifko's room and fell asleep on my new bed like a stone.

9

It was near the middle of the day when I got up. The weather had turned and dirty gray clouds covered the sky. The Iron Gate wind, a bitter wind, was blowing from the east; it whistled through the cracks in the window, and I watched the passers-by shiver and struggle against it. Trifko had gone. I'd missed most of my classes and decided to skip the rest, too.

I was lucky to be done with that kennel just then and to have a room to call my own. The chimney from the kitchen went through our wall and made it nice and warm. But instead of sitting in the window sill, reading, as I had looked forward to with immense pleasure for at least a week, I went out to pound the streets as if I were still homeless.

I remember that wind-swept hike, the little bare trees in front of our school where I went by for no reason, their thin branches waving sadly in all directions; the station square with its cab drivers and porters huddled together under the portico, smoking their self-rolled cigarettes with their backs against the wind; and the riverbank where the choppy waves blew strips of spray over the path. I felt great affection for our shaggy little capital which would bring an ironic smile to the face of a visitor from Paris or New York, and I stood a long time at the water's edge, chewing on the bun I had bought, and with tears in my eyes from the wind.

A couple of years before, I had been on a school outing from Sarajevo, up the Bjelasnica Mountain above the village where my brother is building his sawmill. When we came out of the forest onto the bare rock, we had to walk or crawl across a ledge. It was wide enough, but on one side the ground fell steeply away to a meadow, so far down that you couldn't tell if the little dots in it were sheep or cows. The older boys told us there was nothing to it: the trick was simply to look ahead or to the left, never into the abyss.

Of course it wasn't simple.

Once they told you that, every muscle in you started pulling your head to the right to look precisely in the forbidden direction. And not just with fear; you felt a strange temptation to tumble down into that valley, to jump, as if that wouldn't have meant getting killed but freeing yourself.

On that walk all over Belgrade, just such a sensation accompanied me. I studied the river, I looked at the people hurrying by, last year's leaves whirling through the gutter, heavy chimney smoke swept low into the street by the wind, and all that time I was avoiding looking down into a kind of precipice at my side. It was of course in my mind only, but I wasn't being fanciful. It felt precisely like that crawl on the Bjelasnica ledge.

There was a void near me, and I had to concentrate intently on the day around me in order not to be drawn toward it.

10

That void was connected with the newspaper clipping. But I didn't try to think it through, not then.

Of the Serbian papers, only one little weekly took up the item about the supposed June 28 visit of the Archduke. It was Cabri again who brought it in and read it to us. By way of comment, the magazine printed parts of a letter by Zerajic, that student in the unmarked grave. A few days before his death, Zerajic had written that Sarajevo looked as if it were "a damned and doomed town, everyone bowing, everyone bowing down. . . . With pain I must say, this is blasphemy against history." That was about the visit to Sarajevo by the Emperor Francis Joseph, in 1910.

"Oh, yes—I remember how they kept his moves a secret till the last moment," Djula said, "and they then whisked him through with half the army standing by to make quite sure no one could as much as spit in the direction of our Franjo Josip, Francesco Giuseppe."

Cabri put the magazine down in the middle of the billiard table. "If it's true, though," he said, "that they're sending us this Francis Ferdinand now, Sarajevo should show him that some of us have stopped bowing."

"The man hates us already, anyway. What would be the point? They don't believe that loyalty stuff in Vienna themselves. That's for the gallery."

"You cannot be sure," Cabri said. "Our rulers have a great capacity for hypnotizing themselves with their own words."

Djula answered, "Suppose you stage a demonstration; the police and the soldiers will heave you out of sight before you've properly opened your mouth. Francis Ferdinand would never even notice, and they'd be bound not to enlighten him."

"But if he did hear," Trifko said, "or if you'd succeed in blocking the route that he . . ."

"Impossible."

"And what if you did? 'A Serbian anarchist disturbance.' And he'd see a lot of loyal citizens shake their fists at us for embarrassing them as hosts to His Excellency. And after that we'd be in jail for a month or two."

"A year or two," I inserted.

"We're achieving things right now here in Belgrade," someone said, "we're making our people aware of politics. I believe in Masaryk's program, 'realistic tactics, day-to-day work.' This is a long-term struggle."

"But our lives aren't long term," Trifko said, "that's the trouble. Our lives are short term. This very second one man is humiliated, one child is starving to death, one woman—"

He fell silent.

"We are focused on the future," the man who had quoted Thomas Masaryk said. "Our work goes beyond ourselves."

Cabri had been nodding his head through all of this, as if each and every word spoken confirmed an idea of his own.

"Oh, fuck it!" he cried. "I don't know . . . listen, this twentieth century of ours still has eighty-six years to go, eight and six-tenths dreary decades ahead of us for chipping, like birds at a rock, chipping away at the self-satisfied greed of our leading citizens, and at the dumb . . . the dumb dumbness of the rest of us—Oh, God," he ended, and walked out.

I stood up, I thought I'd follow him. But just then he came back into the café and walked to the billiard table to pick up his magazine. There had been a game in progress before this, and the players had now started up again, putting his magazine aside, on top of the stove, which was not lit.

Somehow this made Cabri livid. He stood there with that weekly in his hand, glaring, and then he swept it and the billiard balls with it across the table. "Billiard players," he muttered and marched out again.

I walked out after him, but as I stood in the doorway and saw him cross the market square, I didn't follow him.

What would I say to him? That I understood his reaction? That he was a fine fellow and that billiard playing wasn't what the times called for? It'd be a very useless speech. I would have to say—but no, I wouldn't. I shook my head to fight off some kind of panic threatening me.

I didn't want to talk to Cabri.

I rounded the corner and set out for the monastery but after a couple of blocks I didn't want to go there any more either. To hell with it. I had put five dinar in my pocket that morning (meant to last a week).

11

When I got back to my room, Trifko was reading in bed. He had rigged a piece of string from his bed post to the cord of the lamp, in order to pull it from the middle of the ceiling over to his corner. He didn't have enough light to read by otherwise: the landlord had put a very dim bulb in there. Trifko got up to undo the knot, but I said I didn't mind being in the shadows. I lay on my bed and stared at the ceiling. "What's the matter with you?" he asked. "Nothing, why?" "You seem miserable."

He surprised me. I had thought that I'd got rid of my un-easiness and that I felt quite content, in an admittedly stupid way, having come home from a four-dinar meal with a lovely taste of gravy still in my mouth and the smell and the warmth of the log fire they had in the restaurant still on my clothes and hands.

" 'A haze,' " Trifko read out. " 'She saw things through a haze, peculiar to persons very ill, or carried away by some all-absorbing, great idea.' "

He was reading Andreyev, *The Seven Who Were Hanged.* " 'She felt boundless love, boundless eagerness to do great deeds, and boundless contempt for herself.' . . . She was a revolutionary, of course," he told me. "I don't think I under-stand that contempt stuff."

"No, I don't understand either. 'Boundless contempt'? At least not in that one sentence you read. I'd think you'd have to believe very much in yourself to plan great deeds. Please let me read it after you."

"Contempt, maybe, for profiting . . . you know, like that man who cried, 'There are no innocents,' that Paris anarchist. No matter what you do, it isn't enough, that idea," Trifko said.

"But if they hanged her for what she was doing . . . What more can you ask? They are all hanged, aren't they?"

"I haven't read that far yet," he answered, "but I'm sure. Andreyev doesn't play tricks; it's no Nick Carter."

We never returned that book to the school library. I carried it with me for weeks, and there are pages in it I well-nigh know by heart.

I thought about that mysterious, contemptuous girl, whom I saw as my Sophia, or as the Sophia Perovskaya after whom she was modeled, and I brooded about her motives and her fate as if she weren't existing only in Andreyev's mind but was real, pacing up and down in the cell of a Czarist prison.

I drafted the message that I'd send her, that would reconcile her with herself; you believe in love, I would write, you have a right not to be that severe with yourself. I wouldn't write of a silent, eternally sunlit, ice-cold universe but about a world

filled with compassionate love, born from the simple discovery
that we are all such lost creatures on this earth, that if we
don't dry each other's tears, there's nothing left to choose or
to hope for.

I'd think about this and be near crying for her.

12

My talk with Cabri.

We ended up in an orgy of talking. Suddenly and without
planning it, he and I started spending long wet evenings in
Kalemegdan Park together. We'd walk around and around the
path that circles the fountain, the pebbles crunching under our
feet and the rain dripping on us from the trees, in the dark,
with every hundred feet or so a cone of light from a gas lamp.
Then we'd wipe the seat of a bench dry with a sleeve of our
jackets and sit, our legs stretched out, listening to the silence,
and within that silence the sound of water everywhere (except
in the fountain, which always stood dry), and rarely the steps
of another visitor, usually a man with a dog. We'd follow them
with our eyes and never utter a word until the dark had swallowed them up again. The April rains had come in earnest,
and there is an image in my mind now of a string of rainy
days and evenings fused together, one like the other. We never
said we'd come back the next day, we just ended up doing so.
I could draw that bench facing the fountain, with its rusty
iron curlicue supports and the scarred green wood in which
dozens of initials had been scratched. How I wish I were sitting
there right now! Oh, God. Or, oh, fuck it.

We talked about life, about ourselves, our parents (his were
very different from mine; his father had burned all Cabri's
books), about the world, about action, and about silly things
too. We weren't gloomy. I don't mean to give that impression;
a bit vague and wistful. When we talked about when we would
have liked to live, we both said, "Earlier, or later." Say around

1789, when the world was so full of expectation, or at some future date, who knows when, when things will be better than they are now.

"We're in an iron age," Cabri said, "and so many people don't even realize we cannot go on like this." And I looked at that peaceful scene, the evening mist over the trees with its yellow reflections of the gaslight, and wondered, was it really that bad? Yes, it was. Yes, it is. A whitened sepulcher.

And then Cabri would bend over and pick up a handful of pebbles and drop them one by one and try to kick them away in mid-air, and with each kick he'd whisper urgently, "Act! Act! Deeds!" Oh, yes, he said, he perfectly understood my indifferent-universe idea, perhaps that was all there was to it—but perhaps not, and shouldn't we make sure not to give ourselves the benefit of the doubt and not take the passive and easy way out? "History proves . . ." Cabri said, and my thoughts went on a side road.

In that moment I saw brightly and, it seemed to me then, with startling originality, that history, nationalisms, symbolisms, languages, the races of man, countries, war and peace, all our institutions, churches, courts, senates, barracks, beliefs, taboos, all the rules of all our games, were indeed but that: rules of games. A tiny bunch of organisms, human beings, living on an obscure planet, had by the very fact of their interactions brought about certain regularities and predictabilities for their frog pond, ant heap, and had had the arrogance to call these: laws, laws of nature, if you please. A child stealing another child's toy is as serious an event for investigation as Napoleon's retreat from Moscow, for as we supposedly dig into the mysterious logic and illogic of history, we're only tabulating a million children stealing a million toys. We never step outside our own circle, nor can we; that Latin saying about "nothing human is alien to me" is thus particularly boring, it's a truism.

"Do you agree," I asked Cabri, who was looking at me, awaiting the answer to a question I hadn't listened to, "that deep and eternal thoughts and philosophies can by necessity only be in human beings, and are therefore just as undeep and uneternal as a toothache or the urge to pee, and vice versa?"

"Well, yes," he answered immediately, "and so what?"

So what, indeed.

"To get back to the visit of the satrap to Sarajevo," Cabri said (he had taken that expression "satrap" from me). "I want to be there, if it's true. I want to lie in the road if all by myself, or ring a church bell, or unfurl a Serbian flag, something, anything, that is *not* a 'blasphemy against history.' It'll be like a stone in a lake, Gavre, with ever-widening ripples; it'll wake up some people, somewhere. Don't you see?"

"Yes, maybe," I answered.

"What do you mean, maybe?"

"Precisely that. It may be as you say, or it may not be."

It was at the end of an evening when this particular exchange took place, I remember that; the rain had stopped, it had grown cold, and we could see our breaths as we spoke.

Cabri stood up, and I heard him say something about billiard playing. I took hold of his sleeve. He turned toward me, and, jumping into that void, I heard myself say, "What I mean is, the only proper response to his visit, the only action that would be commensurate, would be, to kill him."

I don't remember what Cabri answered, but it was nothing momentous. We made a round of the fountain and then, putting our collars up, we jogged back into the street. He bought me a coffee at a roadside stand. We talked of other things.

13

To kill him.

The satrap, Francis Ferdinand, was standing at the edge of a large clearing in the wood. The ground was hilly and he was looking down into the bluish haze of the tree line. Everything within sight was blue, green, or brown, and he was aware of that and it pleased him. He liked to think of himself as a hunter foremost. It's good to be in a blue-brown-green world, he thought; there is no need for other colors, except for our yellow and red heraldically. The Hungarians, who do everything wrong, have green in their heraldry, which is the one place where it does not belong. My ancestors were forest people, white-fleshed in a green pure world and a different species from the nomads of the dusty, red plains, barbarians, gypsies, wanderers, despoilers. You exaggerate, he then told himself with a smile. My father used to say, our empire is seven cities in an ocean of barbarism. Three, really. I've never even liked Salzburg. But thanks be to God it's not all cities, like England, or like America will soon be. Three cities in a two-hundred-and-fifty-thousand-square-mile hunting preserve; that is a happier description. When I am driven through the streets of Vienna, I am in an artificial situation; tensions, inimical forces are at work everywhere. Standing here, I am in my natural place. I am part of creation, but I have dominion over every living creature in it, as God ordained. Only Jews are at home in cities.

The barbarians hunt with other animals; they set animal against animal, falcon against heron, dog against bear. I don't even like dogs; I am man, and I am alone.

I kill animals but with pleasure and without hatred; they are killed but without rebelliousness. I kill but I preserve, too, as the very word says. Nature can only be in the trust of those who own her, who own the land.

He felt a strange tenderness within himself at that thought.

His gun bearer silently handed him his Mannlicher rifle. The rustling of leaves and the sound of sticks against tree trunks had become audible, which meant that the beaters were again approaching the edge of the clearing. He shouldered his rifle, pleased with the moment of cool touch of the metal against his cheek, the slight smell of weapon oil, and the reassuring feel of the carved wood of the stock. That was the precise excitement of each shot, hard wood and steel on one end, soft skin, tissue, veins, and blood on the other end. A chamois was standing motionless under the trees, almost invisible in the undergrowth, hesitant to come out into the open. His gun bearer looked at him, but he slightly shook his head, for it was a doe. Then, as the beaters came nearer, the doe broke cover and dashed across the clearing, followed by two more does and a buck chamois. Lightly, the hunter fired both barrels, so fast that for one instant both bullets were in flight. The first one struck the chamois in his ear, leaving hardly any trace of entering, flew through his brain and stopped in the wall of the skull. Thus he was across the line of death as the second bullet entered his neck, broke the aorta, and tore through the skin once more, now with less speed and thus making a large wound, arching to the ground a hundred feet away. The animal dropped to his forelegs and then rolled over. The beaters appeared, three men, and stood still awaiting further orders.

The hunter handed his rifle back to the bearer, and they walked over to look at the kill. The bearer took his knife to cut out the animal's testicles which make the flesh musky, but the hunter shook his head. "Never mind that," he said. "This one's too beautiful; I won't have him eaten. Perhaps we'll have him mounted, the whole beast; the children would like that."

Kneeling down, he lifted the animal's head and studied it. "A beautiful beast," he repeated, letting it fall back to the ground. He wiped his hands on the grass. "I think he was the last one here," he said to no one in particular, and walked back to the lodge.

There, the sun had come around to the lawn, and he decided to have his drink outside. He shook his head when his man appeared to pull off his boots. He put his feet up and closed his eyes to the warm light, and started mentally composing his daily letter to his wife.

14

Is the life or death of any one man or woman ever decisive? Isn't it instead deep invisible currents that move us along? We had aimless discussions on it in our secret school-group days, how Tolstoy had said that it wasn't Napoleon but the people who led Europe to Waterloo and how Marx was even more drastic. Then there'd always be someone to ask, why then had Marx bothered to write.

Was Francis Ferdinand important as a *life*? The archduke next in line for the succession supposedly had a less vicious personality. But what difference would that make? A subtle tyranny is worse than a crude one, and lasts longer.

Or, if all these men were but marionettes dangling from the strings of fate, we shouldn't give a damn about them. Maybe just feel pity.

My words to Cabri had had nothing to do with all that. I had known immediately when I read Cabri's newspaper clipping that there'd be no dignity in any action but silence—or death. All those other plans would be schoolboy stuff, a self-serving, embarrassing mess. At that Sarajevo Judas banquet one should remain absent, or overturn the table.

If the satrap would die by setting foot in our capital on our 28th of June, there'd be a rent in that fog in which he played the benevolent ruler and we the loyal citizens. It might even shake up some of those who were long since used to perpetrating their petty tyrannies in the shadow of that vast tyranny.

Tyrannicide. We were at war. As he used force without right in Bosnia, he had put himself in a state of war with Bosnia.

That is from John Locke.

After Zerajic's death, dozens of books had been removed from the school library shelves. One day we found a pack of them in a basement cupboard, wrapped in paper on which was written, "Janitor!—To be destroyed." We took them away and found they were in praise of tyrannicide, Locke, Schiller, and even a Jesuit priest, Mariana. We were intrigued but not specially impressed. The violence of our old world, preached daily as patriotism, was back here in more subtle form. The German poet and his *William Tell*—wasn't he praising the only kind of patriotism possible before there is a fatherland? Would he have written his *Tell* now, in 1914 Berlin?

Our Sarajevo high school rebellion had been a different one. It had been about nothing less than changing a world we rejected, it had been against nothing less than death. It had been precisely against all those schoolbook heroes so ready to kill.

We had been happy that our history was one of victims and sacrifices and that our national anniversaries commemorated defeat.

We may have been tiresome adolescents, "idealists," as an editorial in a Sarajevo paper had written, between quotes, making it into a dirty word. We were even aware of ourselves that way at times.

But we knew that we knew. Once you've seen that a shadow is a shadow and not a rabbit, nobody will be able to convince you otherwise.

We had a philosophy teacher who would ask us one by one if we'd kill a hundred innocent Chinese if we could do so from a distance and without fear of punishment and receive a million crowns for it.

He was a stupid man.

Here was a more virtuous problem: could a murder, even of a vicious satrap, be a revolutionary deed?

And I? Where did I fit in?

I drew a vertical line on a piece of paper and wrote above the left column: "Silent universe." And above the right one: "Brotherly love."

I wrote in the left column: "It is too easy, letting my belief in the absurdity of things be an excuse.

"Two kinds of despair. The cosmic one is a despair de luxe. Of no use. The despair of the peasants of Bosnia is something else. And if I really believe in my silent universe, then nothing should make me afraid, no prospect of anything on earth. Otherwise my philosophy is wobbly. So much more reason then for not using it as a way out."

Under "brotherly love" I wrote: "Kill—for the love of my fellows?"

I did not know what else to write there.

15

On the way to school I passed a commotion in a side street. I heard a lady say, "There's been a bad accident." We never used to go look at things like that, we considered that morbid and beneath our dignity; but now I stood still.

We'd had so many discussions on violence, saying all the usual things. But Milan, who had been through a war, had never opened his mouth on the subject.

I thought, here is a test and I have to pass it.

I turned and shoved my way through a circle of onlookers.

A young man had been run over by an automobile. He was lying on the wet cobblestones, motionless, with his head on a folded-up coat. His wide-rimmed felt hat lay beside him. The chauffeur and everyone else just stood and stared.

The narrow wheels of the car had gone over the lower part of his body, in which front and back wheel had made two separate grooves with almost square corners. No blood was visible: his trousers were pressed into the wounds. His face had a terrifying green, impossible, color.

I hated myself for feeling weak, and kneeling beside the man, I said aloud that we should cut open his clothes. Accepting a pair of scissors a lady brought out of a handbag, I gently cut his trousers from the knee up, without pulling at the material. The blood had assembled within, and it now welled out, raising a muffled "oh" from the people. I stepped over the body and made myself work on the other leg. A voice said, "I'll take over," and a man with a doctor's bag kneeled beside me and tugged the cloth out of the wounds. "He's not dead," he called over his shoulder, "and we can't move him like this; get me bandages. Are you a medical student?" he asked me.

I forced my eyes to focus. Thick, red edges were curling outward from those gaps, and through them a purple mass was visible of membranes and intestines. "Will he live?" I asked the doctor. "God, no," he said, "the aorta is ruptured. And look at that mess," and he pointed where something palpitated. The crowd opened for a man carrying a large ball of lint, and I got out of his way and walked off. Sweat was standing on my forehead and I had to swallow in order not to throw up. That green face, of a man who had been strolling along this same sidewalk a few minutes ago, planning his day perhaps, or his summer or his life. "That's how the face of death looks," I whispered. I didn't feel stronger for my test but weaker. Maybe that is how it had to be.

16

That evening Trifko and I went to the Café Royal to read the papers. He had made friends with the headwaiter. Once a week, we helped out in the billiard room and after that we got free coffees at the reading table in the café. I had left Cabri at the Cornerbar. After those words "to kill him" had been spoken, he and I in silent accord hadn't gone back to the park.

We could have afforded to pay for a coffee, I guess, but this way was much nicer. We'd stay for hours with no waiter staring at us.

"What have you and Cabri been up to?" Trifko asked me.

I wondered what to answer. It would be stupid to act mysterious, but it would be worse to risk getting Trifko involved in something. He was really too young.

"Holy Jesus!" Trifko said.

On the front page of the *Zeit* of that day, or anyway of the most recent copy to arrive, was the news of the Imperial visit to Bosnia and Hercegovina, complete with a picture and a map.

Trifko's German wasn't much but he recognized the key words in it, of course, and at once cut it out with the end of his coffee spoon. He pushed it over to me; we both got up in the same moment to leave. The animated voices in the room, and all those newspapers and illustrated weeklies we had looked forward to reading, now seemed repellent.

Back in our room, I wrote out a translation, and then we both started making copies of it. Why, we didn't quite know. To do something with those hours that had turned sour. Powerlessness, as surely as power, corrupts in the original sense of the word, it spoils.

17

When I woke up at dawn, it was again or still raining. I had a lot of homework, but I just sat in the window sill staring at the text of one of Livy's goddam wars. I'd been so proud my first day in Sarajevo grammar school, I had carried my Caesar with its *De Bello Gallico* title sticking out for everyone to see. That was long ago. The best moment with Livy now came when I realized I was sitting on a big chunk of bread left over from the day before. I went out, chewing on it. Trifko was still asleep.

At eleven that morning, as we changed classrooms for the final hour, a decision in me jelled, I hastily collected my things and slipped out of the building. The school had been stuffy and warm, and it was good to be out in the street, where a fresh wind blew, carrying only occasional sprays of rain. I set out for the government center, the building where Milan worked as a clerk. I was there before twelve, but the porter told me they had already gone to lunch. He pointed out the café where Milan and his colleagues always ate.

Inside that place, in a haze of tobacco and steaming raincoats, loud voices, waiters piling up plates, it took me a while to discover him at a table with two other men. He saw me at the same time and waved me over. "I came to ask your advice," I said, "but I just missed you. When—" "Eat with us," Milan interrupted, "you and I can go for a stroll after." And he very formally introduced me to the two men, who worked in his department. They were talking office gossip and I didn't try to join the conversation; I felt my appearing there had embarrassed Milan, though he would be too nice to show it. They went on to politics then, and those men sounded more sympathetic than I somehow would have expected from their faces. "We're all in the same boat," Milan said in a sort of reassuring way, addressing himself to me.

I smiled at him. I had really been lucky, with my group of friends in Belgrade. I no longer worried whether it had been the right thing to go and see Milan.

"People still reading Andreyev," one of his colleagues half asked, looking at my book.

"Why 'still'?" I said.

"His style is so dated. Among the Russians, the new novelists are so much finer."

"Yes, Andreyev is not well written," the other man added.

I shrugged, but seeing Milan's ironic look at all three of us, I decided not to let them get away with that. Surprised by my own vehemence, I visualized Andreyev (whom I didn't know, of course) as vulnerable, grateful for my defense, and I repeated, "Not well written? What does that signify? Do you think that we read Andreyev the way a fat man eats his dinner? To please our senses? Do you think we read books to be flattered? To recognize our own precious little emotions?"

"Is it wrong to do that?" Milan asked.

"Who cares, it's not what we're after, that's all. We're no longer interested in private gentlemen and ladies analyzing their fine feelings."

"I like fine feelings," one of the men said dryly. "I admire that civilization that for instance is embodied in Paris at this very moment, an example to us Slavs, a magic circle of poetry and art, and concert music, and *belles lettres*."

"I admire it too," I answered, "but the price for it is preposterous. Strikers have to be shot, coolies whipped, miners gassed, and Moroccan villages burned down, just to create that magic circle of nicely dressed people listening with civilized rapture to Bizet."

"Hmm," one of the men said, and the other looked equally unhappy. There was a silence and I felt obliged to say more.

"I don't mean to sound like a fanatic. I don't mean that they should ban or burn your belles lettres."

41

"That's very nice of you."

"Don't you see," I said, "it's just not interesting any more. That supreme egotism that's needed, first, to produce those belles lettres of yours and, second, to appreciate them, was of interest a hundred years ago, when people were just discovering themselves as individuals. But now it's not. Not because human joy and sorrow, individually, alone, aren't important, but because to go on writing that way, there has to be a piece missing in you. Otherwise the horrors of this world couldn't so patently fail to get to you. But who wants descriptions of the world, of anything, from an observer in whom there's a piece left out?"

"Hmm," the first man said again.

"Are you a writer?" the second man asked, registering surprise.

"He's a high school student," Milan answered for me.

"Oh," they both said at the same time.

18

Milan and I set off north along the avenue, against the midday stream of men returning to their work.

"Now tell me why you came here and gave us a lecture, instead of in school listening—" Milan began.

"Oh, damn! Was I embarrassing you?"

Milan put his hand on my shoulder. "I'm joking. I liked it. I've often thought there was a piece missing in those two. What are we to talk about, to show we're different?"

I enjoyed that lead. "About arms," I said with some solemnity.

There was an irrevocable line of commitment I did not want to overstep. I wanted to be vague. "Suppose there was a plan to attack something or someone, a political attack of course. Would there be help for that here, in weapons, or money?"

"Of course not," Milan answered promptly.

I was taken aback. I had expected him to ask questions and to study my face, with approval or disapproval, but at least with interest. But I also realized other feelings were mixed in with my disappointment. Perhaps, I said to myself, I'm cowardly enough to have hoped for objections and obstacles.

Milan didn't look inclined to pursue the matter, yet he went on with our walk, which led away from his office.

"Where did Zerajic get his revolver?" I finally asked.

"I don't know. Not in Serbia, I'm sure."

"And you're the man who's in favor of creating a secret army here."

"An army, yes," Milan answered firmly. "But what you said, sounded more like banditry, or what Marxists call adventurism."

I sighed and stood still. "I'll walk you back to your building," I said.

Milan looked at me. "Listen, friend," he then said, "you know as precisely as I do that Serbia hangs in the balance in this fat world run by Great Powers. We freed ourselves from the Turks, thanks to no one, and the Austrians would now like to gobble us up. After Bosnia, we're next on their list. That's the reason the English were quite happy when we were under heathen Turkey rather than on our own, though they're so Christian, it comes out of their ears. There is no community of interest between a small country and a Big Power, as little as between a poor man and a rich man."

I said, "I don't see what you're getting at."

"If a pebble is thrown against the window of that wicked old man, the Emperor Franjo Josip, and they can prove it was a Serbian pebble, they'd use it as an alibi to put the thumbscrews on this nation and to go to war against it. I personally think they will anyway, and they may have a surprise in store for them when they do. But it's crucial we don't give them an alibi; it's our only chance to keep the others benevolently neutral. Especially that Kaiser of the Germans under his spike helmet, his spare prick as we called it in the army."

We started back toward the government center.

"I know you're not an agent provocateur," Milan went on.

"No, I don't know. I'm ready to stake my life on it, but I cannot swear it to anyone else. I can't swear that you're not out to involve Serbians in some subtle Viennese whipped cream morass of duplicity. So you see—"

"Suppose," I answered, "just an if thing, mind you, just in principle, you were asked to give those hand grenades of yours. They're right there under your bed. No need to swear to anyone about anything."

Milan thought about that. "In principle, the answer is yes," he finally said. "In practice, I'd strongly advise against it. Those grenades weren't too good when they came fresh from the arsenal. We've had one in four or five failing to go off. Or too soon, which is worse. In battle, when a whole battalion was attacking an outpost, they served their purpose. But for what you seem to be thinking of, they'd be a terrible risk. And they've now been in that box for a year. Still—"

We had come to Milan's entrance gate. Everyone had gone in and it was very quiet there. The porter who had told me where to find Milan's café, was sweeping the courtyard. When he saw us together, he nodded to affirm the success of his directions, and I nodded back at him.

"Do you, do those people you're 'in principle' talking for, know how to handle hand grenades?" Milan asked softly.

"No."

"Can they shoot a pistol?"

"No."

Milan laughed. "If you're an agent provocateur, you're sure a terrible one. I have to go in now or they'll fire me."

"Yes. Thanks for the cabbage soup."

"We'll talk about it again," Milan said and unexpectedly added, "Also, I'm a very good weapons instructor."

19

And the very next evening, Milan took me aside in the Cornerbar.

"Tell those people you mentioned yesterday, those If people, to come to Kosutnjak Park tomorrow at five, at the north entrance."

When I showed up, Milan was already there. "Are you the sum total of the If persons?" he asked.

"What are we going to do?"

"You'll see."

Milan led the way, walking fast, across a swampy lawn, ending up in a neglected corner of Kosutnjak. Here the leaves weren't raked, a fallen tree was rotting in the middle of the path, and there were little hills everywhere from moles or some such creatures. "Look at that oak," Milan said and he pointed at a dead tree with a short, oddly shaped trunk. "Do you see, it looks like a man. Stand here and try." And he put his hand in his jacket and came out with a pistol. "Push the catch off. Alright. Hold it rigid like this. Point at the tree, and pull."

I did as he said, there was an explosion, and the pistol made a vicious jump in my hand, almost making me drop it.

"That went nowhere," Milan said. "Again."

I held it better that time, and went on firing. After four times, there was only a click. I took the pistol in my left hand and shook the pain out of my right hand.

"It holds six bullets," Milan said, "but we never put in more than four. If you compress the spring too much, the bullets don't come straight out of the clip and may jam as they're shoved into the chamber. It's not a very new pistol. I'll show you how it works."

"What do F and S mean?" I asked.

" 'Feuer' and 'Sicher.' That's 'off' and 'on' for the safety catch. It's a Browning, but it was made for the German army, that's why it's in German. The first bullet is put in the chamber by pulling this part back with one hand, holding on with the other. The rest go in automatically, through the reaction force. Here's four more. You put them in, and let's see you hit the tree now. Take sight along the barrel, don't try to shoot like a bandit. And look, only when it's cocked, when you've put a bullet in the chamber, is this metal point down, and the line of sight unobstructed. You can always tell."

45

That afternoon, I hit the trunk a couple of times from about forty yards, and Milan hit it every time. We went on till it got dark.

"We'll come back here same time day after tomorrow," Milan said. "I must hold on to the pistol, I promised."

And thus, without having been asked what it was all about, and even without any decision sharp in my own mind, I was started on pistol practice in Kosutnjak Park, the very place where the Serbian Michael III had been ambushed and murdered on arrangement from Vienna, half a century before.

The next time, Milan again asked, "Are you all the If persons?" and when I laughed, he said, "That's not right. Think about it. If one's serious about an action, any action, you need reserves, people to fall back on, to share the risk and to make the odds more favorable."

I had thought about it but I was waiting. I could do or undo anything within my own mind. Once I went beyond that, I had to be damn well free of doubt.

That afternoon I hit the tree three times out of eight.

We were going to try from farther away then, but we heard voices, and decided to leave. "We'll come back on Monday," Milan said, "Saturday afternoon and Sunday are too risky."

At the Cornerbar, Djula suddenly asked me, "Why do you keep sniffing at your hand? It looks revolting." They all laughed and I blushed but didn't answer.

I hadn't realized I was doing that. My hand smelled of gunpowder, a strange disturbing smell. The smell of battlefields. Or maybe I just imagined it.

20

When I hit our tree almost every shot at forty yards and half the time at sixty yards, Milan made me try it while running. It was difficult but I had a few hits. He tried it twice and hit the tree the second time. After that, we sat on a rock and he showed me how to clean the Browning.

"You can keep it now," he said. "Remember, you may just give it back to me, and no one will question you why. But please make very sure it's not seen."

He loaded it and handed it to me. I put it inside my shirt, the barrel secured in my belt. "I could lay my hands on more cartridges," Milan went on, "and maybe another pistol. Also a couple of good hand grenades if we want them. We can hardly practice with those, but I can explain them."

I thanked him.

An odd feeling, walking back through town with the metal against my skin. An armed man. And this was Belgrade. How would that feel within the Austrian border!

I put the Browning under my mattress, tucked in a sock. Knowing it was there, with the knowledge to use it—I could still feel the power of its recoil in the muscles of my hand—was like having passed another test.

I was climbing up a stairway; I saw it as a wide marble flight of steps, as in the picture of a Roman temple. The automobile victim had been one step up; facing him, I mean. This was another.

Now there was a break in my life. A pause. I looked around me again, heard the professors in school, studied lessons, and wandered down the streets in the lengthening evenings. There seemed to be weddings all over the place, and almost every evening I went past a restaurant garden where wedding guests were dancing in a circle in the Eastern Orthodox fashion.

The sun set farther and farther north, over the undulating plain that is called Szeben by the Austrians and has for its real name Srem, behind the Sava River. Each night it set in blood-red clouds, long afterward reflected in the water. Then the Austrian-Hungarian lights of Zemun started to flicker through the dark blue dusk along the horizon.

Perhaps I was just more aware of that spring. The air was so soft, and there was a temptation in everything, a sweetness in everything feminine.

Because of that, to break that spell, I didn't wait any longer.

I took Cabri back to our park bench, and before I had said a word, he asked, "Have you been brooding about June 28?"

"Yes."

"To kill him?"

"Yes."

"Can I be in on it with you?" he asked.

"I was going to ask you. We have to be very sure."

"Trifko wants to join," Cabri said. "He guessed."

"I like him very much," I answered, "but he is so young. I was going to ask Djula—that is, if you and I decided we wanted another man."

"But Trifko really knows already," Cabri said, "and he's not too young. He's as cool as an old general."

Cabri got up and stroked the rough stone of the fountain. "We may die," he remarked.

"Do you think we have the right to try and kill this man?" I asked.

"Yes. Don't you?"

"I still don't know," I answered.

"Do you know where to get arms and money?"

"Arms, yes," I told him. "Money, I don't know yet."

"We'll cook up something," Cabri said. "We must also try to lay our hands on poison." "For ourselves," he ended after a moment's pause.

I shivered, but not with fear.

"If one of us gets caught, he won't want to betray the others," Cabri said. "And when you think of it—none of us would want to be at the mercy of the Austrian police."

I didn't answer.

"It wouldn't be realistic to assume that we'd escape," Cabri insisted. "Hadn't you felt that?"

I swallowed. "I had thought that maybe I wouldn't want to escape," I finally said.

Another silence. I didn't know if he understood me, but he didn't ask and thus I said no more.

"Let's shake hands on it," he said. "And then go and tell Trifko. We must swear an oath."

That made me smile. "We can swear to silence if you want," I answered, "but to no more than that. I want you and Trifko to feel free, even in Sarajevo, to change your mind."

"And what about you?"

"I am sure now. But I'd feel frightened if I had bound you two."

"You didn't. You don't. What goes for us, has to go for you too."

"Well, we're all free then."

We walked back, and looking at Cabri's face in the light of the street lamps hurt me. He seemed ridiculously young. He looked back at me. "Don't worry about us," he said. "It's not as if we had a choice, is it?"

"No. We have no choice."

21

I lay in bed in the middle of the night and felt my heart pounding like a train engine, I could hear the blood pulse in my ears. My doubt had come back and it made me sick, literally, as if I'd throw up.

I closed my eyes and tried to visualize myself pulling out the Browning and shooting the satrap. But I could not force that scene into any Sarajevo setting I knew. I could only visualize him standing in front of the oak tree in Kosutnjak Park, in fact as mysteriously being that tree. Then I could shoot. A grenade was easier, although I had never seen one explode. I could picture myself at a window; below me the cortege went by and I pulled out the pin, counted, four? ten? and dropped it on that man as he was waving and bowing at an empty street. He shattered as if he himself had exploded.

I was trembling, and I forced myself to lie motionless. I listened to Trifko's regular breathing. He was indeed a brave boy. Then I went back to that carriage and saw it strewn with pieces of uniform and flesh, carpeted with them; and the coachman was driving on as if nothing had happened.

But the soldiers who had been lining the route were now all flocking together in front of my door. They broke it down and as I retreated from my window, I heard their boots in the corridor, doors opening, shrieks of women and children, men shouting. I climbed up the ladder to the roof, jumped over to the next house, and ran on and on.

Then I saw myself in some other room, a friend's, shaving off my mustache, dyeing my hair, and putting on peasant clothes. I came out into an empty, cold, no, sun-baked street. I was cleverly carrying some chickens, their dangling heads dripping blood. I walked to the station.

A crowd filled the station square; I could see them from afar. Over their heads towered those wooden triangles I had seen as a child in 1908: gallows. They were revenging themselves on Sarajevo.

I fell asleep, for now I dreamed that I was in the carriage, that I was the target, and I saw the grenade slowly fall down on me, not as if it had been thrown from a window, but as if it were falling straight from the zenith of the deep blue sky.

It touched me and then it lay in my lap, or stood, rather, purring like a top. I woke up with a cry.

Then I thought that there was no reasoning possible that justified murder. Any such reasoning would imply one life to be worth more than another. It would negate love and our common—our common something or other. If I wanted to do away with this man, if I took that right upon myself, I would have to be ready to die with him. Only in accepting that sacrifice would the insoluble contradiction be solved. To kill for the love of my fellow men.

Hold on now, I said to myself. I don't really believe all that. Why couldn't we claim the right to declare his life of less value than ours, of negative value, forfeited? What set man apart if not his knowledge of good and evil—not an absolute knowledge, not the Garden of Eden one; simply the good and evil of his frog pond, the same level of values that a frog has which declares moisture good, dryness evil.

That simple.

As Cabri had said, there was no choice. Some wheel of fate goes round and round, and as bad luck would have it, my generation was once more a fateful one. We had to.

And then again, and yet, murdering this man and then

running was not justifiable. *Because it did not fit.* We did not want this man away, we wanted more.

We wanted his death as an example.

We wanted to enact for Sarajevo and the world a mystery play, a justice play.

To fire a pistol at this archduke or throw a grenade at him and then hide, wouldn't be enough. Whoever killed him should be ready to die with him. Like the Russian students who had a bomb for their Czar that worked within two or three feet only, killing them as it killed him. Not because his life was worth as much as theirs, but because it was worth infinitely less.

As soon as I had reasoned this far, as soon as I had understood that, I felt a total calm descend on me and I fell into a dreamless sleep.

22

Trifko and Cabri both turned out to want a solemn pact sworn to by us three. Cabri said it should be done in Kosutnjak Park, on the precise spot where Michael III had been knifed to death in that ambush of the year 1868. Cabri was always intensely aware of how things "would look," of the historical protocol, so to speak, that should govern his actions. Trifko just said it would be good luck to go there. The Habsburgs had caused Michael to die under those trees, and that made a good omen for one of that House to become a target in his turn.

As for me, I was rather snooty about the whole business. I pooh-poohed it and said I didn't want to play games. To my taste, it smacked too much of folksy ballads. That kind of thing made me uncomfortable and bored me.

But as those two insisted, we did go to Kosutnjak Park and looked for the lime trees where Michael had died. Cabri found them. At least he claimed they were the lime trees, and there we swore and clasped hands, and in the end I was glad we did.

For, standing in the twilight, I began to understand that they both distilled a lot of natural courage and calm out of their putting themselves back in the past like that. Things were easier for them, once they could compare what they did to some legendary act. I couldn't do this; I was too aware of *thought*, of history being a history of thought. Even as a grade school boy, Saint-Just had been my hero and not Napoleon. I was too much aware that there was something slightly ridiculous about our heroes with their daggers and poems—though I loved them and literally so. But I wanted to be taken terribly seriously both by the peasant villages and by Sir Edward Grey in the London Foreign Office. My own courage had to come from an idea.

Yet because of Trifko and Cabri, because of their way of living with things, because of the Kosutnjak grass on which we stood—"they say every now and again a red blade of grass appears here, from Michael's blood," Trifko said—I wasn't alone with my idea, and it didn't become brittle and barren. They made it natural and in harmony.

I stuck to my plan that they should remain free in their decision, and they accepted, once I agreed I could change my mind, too. I did not need that, though. I felt free within the choice I had already made. For the first time in years, our helplessness was not nagging at me. We were going to do something about it, all we could, and that took the curse off it. I would have preferred living a "normal life," but where would one have to hide to do that?

Thus we, each of us in turn, said, "I swear to the Sarajevo conspiracy."

Looking back on that evening now, I know that our enemies as well as our friends thought that we were grim and fanatic. Sworn assassins. The word spells rage: assassin, hashashin, a hashish-drugged wild man. In reality we were pleased and calm. Once out into the street, we decided to go to some café where we'd never been and no one knew us. We ended up across the freight yard in a place full of night workers drinking coffee dosed with plum brandy, and we got very loud and gay. Then Trifko and I walked Cabri to his room, and then he us to ours, and so on; we didn't seem able to say good night and separate.

Here we were, three boys ready to end our lives within about ten weeks from that day.

It was a mystery. It still seems one to me now.

Did we maybe not really believe it would come to pass?

I know young people aren't supposed to believe in death for themselves. But I think we did. I did. And it took my breath away.

I can only explain it, to myself, by a comparison. Those of our parents, those of the citizens of Sarajevo, who were most shaped or misshaped by the greed and cruelty of the state, who profited and were stained by its violence, were most afraid for their own safety and most afraid to die.

There is a precise mirror image to our mood.

23

Money. We'd need money for traveling to Sarajevo and for staying there. The less money you have, the more conspicuous you are to the police. For money we would go to the money men.

Among the people who controlled business in Belgrade, some originated from Bosnia and Hercegovina, and Trifko and I picked ourselves a prosperous one. He had a whole row of silk entrepôts, an Austrian-Turkish trade that passes through Serbia. It was easy enough to get to see him in his office in the back of a warehouse, but as soon as we said we were asking a subscription for "a political cause," he shouted, "Get out! I don't want to be involved." Then he came after us to make sure we wouldn't accost anyone else there, and when we looked back we saw him standing at the gate in his shirt sleeves, talking to his workmen with arms flailing. "He's going to sic 'em onto us," Trifko said.

That was not the method. It was better to skip the truth, and we ended up taking our collection for "a privately endowed educational project in Bosnia." Cabri's idea, of course. He typeset and printed one letterhead himself, complete with a seal he borrowed from the advertisement of a military tailor in his paper, and he typed a letter under it, signed illegible. I had qualms about using money destined by its donors for such a fine purpose, but these vanished when I found out how hard it was to get any. I seemed to have overestimated that grandeur of those men.

We tried every evening. Trifko was best at it and I worst. I didn't look convincing and was even threatened with the police. We learned not to hesitate or even smile when we showed our letter and made our speech. Then we began to believe in that letter ourselves and as the evenings wore on, to get more and more indignant at the general indifference. We were standing in doorways, and those ex-Bosnians had us sent away by the maid or appeared out of their cosy rooms with a dinner napkin tucked in their vests and muttered something about no change, or fished out half a dinar. Once I got so mad at a lady who produced a two-cent piece that she gave me ten dinar instead, then slammed the door in our faces. When we had worked down the list, we had collected one hundred and ten dinar which we changed into a hundred Austrian crowns and put in a special box.

The three of us stayed together most of our free time after that. Because we were slightly ill at ease with the others, not because we wanted to go on talking about our plans. Those were stored away now like our crowns. At first, in that unreal in-between time, Cabri and I were very nervous; I told them in the Cornerbar I was worried about my coming exam. As for Trifko, he seemed as calm and slept as soundly as ever.

Gradually, we got used to our state of suspense, a suspense between the dailiness of our lives and a date, June 28. Milan helped; he didn't ask anything, but a kind of comforting strength emanated from him. Djula made me ill at ease.

That man, who welcomed me so happily on my first day in Belgrade, now looked at me with a puzzled frown. He thought I'd let him down. I wanted to tell him what we were up to, how he had been my choice, how I wished he were in on it.

But then, it's not a game, it would gratuitously put him in danger later.

One evening he suddenly stood up as Trifko and I were leaving. "I'll walk you home," he said.

A silent procession.

"You two should know," he finally said, "that there are many of us, here and at home in Sarajevo . . . not, not that there's anything so special about that, of course, Slavs have always had plenty of collective courage, in a bunch we're ready for, for great deeds— It's private courages that are needed if we're ever to turn things in a better direction—"

"Yes," I said.

"Yes, that's true," Trifko said.

We walked another silent block.

And then I shouted, "Dammit all, Trifko, what's the point in doing anything if we can't trust our closest friends; how are you going to go on chatting about the fucking future if right here in this group we can't even—I mean, don't we even have the Twelve Just Men—"

I was confused and said no more.

Trifko sighed a very loud sigh and said, "You're right."

We all stood still. "Listen, Djula," I told him, "this is what."

But he interrupted me. He held up his hand. "Stop it," he said. And in his old, cheerful voice, "I thank you both. I understand. I don't want to know. The less talked about, the better. Just remember you can count on me if you ever need me."

"Thank you, Djula," I finally said.

"Thank you," from Trifko.

Djula enveloped us both in that smile of his. "Sleep well," he said. And then quite solemnly, "Allahu khairun hasadan . . ." and more, too difficult to remember. "That is from the Koran, for good luck in a holy battle."

He vanished into the dark.

In our room, Trifko and I made a face at each other: we were embarrassed but didn't admit it. Then I reopened a letter I'd written to Sophia and meant to mail the next day. I tried to read it through her eyes. Was there a change of tone, as Djula had discovered a change? Would the proper, disciplined thing now be not to write and not even to see her back in Sarajevo?

That would be a struggle. But it would be a worse struggle to act natural and cook up some simple reason for being back.

Yet, I realized, that's the way we'd have to do it, for we were not going to try and hide.

24

It was such a very short while since that first day in Belgrade, marking time, waiting to find out about the town and its ways and mysteries, a vast array of discoveries to be made. I had had an old town plan with me, given to me by Sophia. It wasn't very practical, for it had been made a long time back just after the liberation from the Turks, but it was beautiful, drawn on paper glued to linen and colored by hand. Light pink meant Moslem habitations, yellow, Serbians, and purple, Jews, for each house and each fountain was separately marked. Green, for gardens, dominated then. On one house the owner's name had been put, Captain Mischo; why, it was hard to guess. On that map the town gates still existed, the South Gate, where now the theater stands, was still given its old name, "Constantinople Gate." The avenue across town leading toward it, what's now Vase Carapico, was Constantinople Street. The idea of a town gate named for its destination, seven hundred miles off along impossible roads, weeks of hard travel, had fascinated me. I belong to the East; I had been waiting for Belgrade and Serbia to disclose themselves to me.

And now, so soon after, it was already over. No point any more for me in trying to learn more about a country we would soon leave for good.

There had not been one day in which I had lived here, neither just arriving nor about to part. Or, to be honest, maybe one or two.

It was something that made me feel sorry for myself.

It had been like a climb followed immediately by a steep descent back down. No rest in between, no view from the top.

25

I went to visit Skerlic.

One intention carried out, one expectation fulfilled. Touches of self-pity and superstition. But also because it was right and because it gave more solidity to that scattered time, already becoming unreal.

Skerlic had been a hero of ours when we were in school in Sarajevo, an odd role for a professor. He was at the University of Belgrade, one of the few who wrote about the South Slavs in a real, unsloppy way, a people as of now bound only by a common language. "Ideas are worth as much as the men who advocate them" was one of our favorite quotes from him. He was a brave man. When the Croat rebel students fled to Serbia in 1912, he stood at the gate of the university to welcome them. Every word he had written was proscribed in the Austrian Empire. I had meant to become a student of his the following year.

That wasn't going to be.

I wanted to have laid eyes on him, though.

When I rang his doorbell, I didn't know what reason to give for my visit. But the housekeeper who opened the front door didn't ask; she showed me into a room and said to wait. There were two other men there. No one spoke.

My turn came and she led me along a dark passage and opened a curtained door. "Don't stay more than a few minutes," she said.

I had not known he was sick. I found myself in a bedroom. Near the window, in the sunlight, Skerlic was lying on a couch, covered with a blanket. He looked like the portrait in his books, not ill, but his eyes were closed. "Sit here," he said when he heard my footsteps.

I sat on the chair beside him and waited for him to speak but he did not say another word.

Then I thought I should tell him who I was, why I was there, and what he meant to us. And I felt an irresistible need to tell him of our conspiracy—in spite of our oath. But when I had said, "I'm Gavrilo Princip, from Bosnia," he opened his eyes and looked at me, a bright and untired look. He half smiled, and then he nodded as if I had asked him a crucial question and his answer was, "I know it all, and it is well." I smiled back, and he pressed my hand and held it a while. Then he nodded a good-bye and I got up and left.

He died that same week. If it had not been for our conspiracy, I wouldn't have visited him, I wouldn't have been a moment in his life. A good sign, fate approving our plan.

The day after his death, someone I didn't know came up to me after school and said, "We'd like you to carry the wreath of Young Bosnia in Professor Skerlic's funeral. Are you willing?" I don't know why they chose me.

On a warm May day I carried the wreath of flowers with ribbons in the colors of Bosnia, in a long row of men and women walking from the university to the cemetery. All the students were there, Serbian flags and red flags, and no priest.

I thought about Skerlic but without sadness.

I looked into the faces of the inhabitants of Belgrade lining our route, and tried to think myself part of them, and they part of me, to preserve a link, to not leave totally and forever.

26

We left Belgrade on May 28.

Precisely one month to go.

We carried four pistols, cartridges, six hand grenades, and a bottle which, we were told, contained prussic acid though it was yellow rather than colorless. Later we knew that it had been an unnecessary load, plus an unnecessary and terrible risk, smuggling such an arsenal into Austria-Hungary—a risk that would prove fatal to some. But at the time we had a highly exaggerated idea of what the situation in Sarajevo would be like and foresaw ourselves battling our way through half an army battalion. With extra weapons we could muster more support on the spot. Mostly, however, the three of us simply hadn't had the experience or maybe the will power not to accept all of what had been offered to us with such a show of sacrifice.

Milan's source, he had told us, was the underground organization "Unity or Death," of which we all knew. He also had contact with another group that called itself "Life or Death," and Trifko's little joke "When are they going to choose?" didn't amuse Milan at all. These were committed men, he said, and the Serbian civil authorities were by now so worried about provoking Austria that they would have shown them little mercy if they could lay hands on them. We should appreciate their trust. Thus, when Milan came to our room lugging a box that contained no fewer than six hand grenades, heavy, rectangular cast-iron machines, it wasn't as if he were the baker and we could have said, "Fine, we'll take two."

The grenades were clumsy things, of Turkish invention, I wouldn't be surprised, and they didn't seem more reliable to me than those in Milan's room. They had brass caps that had to be unscrewed, looking like curtain knobs, and that bared a detonator which you had to strike on a hard surface. Then they exploded at the count of twelve. Who could stand with a thing like that in his hand for something like ten seconds, within reach of an archduke? But Cabri and Trifko, who had had only an hour or so of pistol shooting at the oak tree, liked them.

Each of us was to transport across the border two grenades, around our middle under our jackets, Trifko and I the four pistols, Cabri the ammunition and the bottle of prussic acid.

We also had the name of a contact, an army officer serving in the Frontier Guards in the river town Sabac. He didn't know of our plans, but he had helped Bosnian students across the border before. We were to introduce ourselves to him only with the letters "M.C." on a piece of paper. These were Milan's initials. I wondered if that was really going to work.

We shared two hundred dinar between us: the "education fund" money in crowns, plus Cabri's savings from his wages, plus an eighteen-dinar contribution by me. Ten left from Sophia's cross. Eight from my coat.

My next to last day in Belgrade, as I was sorting out my stuff, I had suddenly eyed that coat as if it were a ghost. It was old, of heavy wool, made for our winters; the thought struck me that I would not ever need it again and I started to tremble. Then I pulled myself together, jumped up, and took it to the pawnshop in Dorcol, where they gave me eight dinar for it. Everything else I owned, only books really, I decided to take with me to Sarajevo.

At the school, my last afternoon, I told the dean that an illness in my family called me away. That would avoid inquiries when I didn't show up any more. And at the Cornerbar they gave us a farewell dinner.

No point in keeping our departure a secret from them. We said we wanted to be in Bosnia for the summer and were traveling together. They assumed we had some plan or other, for they all toasted us and they didn't ask when we'd be back. We weren't trying to be mysterious, just protecting ourselves and them by keeping our mouths shut. I won't deny it was rather grim and miserable, my last day in school, only a few weeks away from the final exam that was to have gotten me into the university. And that dean listening superciliously to my family illness story. Those dark, long corridors and stuffy classrooms seemed very important and secure, and I memorized for myself how they looked.

The morning of May 28, Trifko and I were awake at the first light. We wrapped our things, tied those grenades around our waists, which was tricky for they had no grooves and were slippery, took them off again, sat around, and finally at six and much too early, softly left the house.

It was cold in the streets and the river was hidden under a morning fog. We walked to the river port. The first stage of our journey was by boat, the little steamer from Belgrade to Sabac; there's no train there.

We got to the pier more than an hour ahead of time. Cabri had come even earlier; we saw him waiting for us on a bench and we shook hands without speaking. Our tickets were as deck passengers, and we filed aboard as soon as someone undid the rope across the gangplank. Putting our bundles together near the railing, Trifko and Cabri sat down on two bollards and I leaned over the rail and stared at the town.

We were tied up right next to the railway bridge where I had come in, on that dawn morning, and had decided never to go back. New people would be standing there tomorrow and have their first look at the flag of Serbia.

The fog lifted, the sun shone over the water. Peasants with empty baskets and sacks, returning from the markets, were coming aboard, plus an occasional traveler in city clothes who vanished into the midship saloon. Peddlers made the rounds with cigarettes and coffee urns. The fortress, and the towers and minarets of Belgrade stood out sharply against the sky, no longer milky now but summer blue. The two gendarmes who had been pacing up and down near the gangplank—no occasion is complete without policemen picking their teeth and watching—came aboard. A sharp toot from the steam whistle.

An old man, who had been sitting on a bollard on the quay, slowly got up and undid the hawser. He dragged it across the cobblestones, with a grin at the deckhand who stood beside me. I can still see his face and that grin; he had only a couple of teeth left. Then, with an awkward heave, he tossed the hawser onto our deck.

The boat suddenly trembled from bow to stern as the engine started up. It belched smoke and turned its nose against the stream. "We're off," Cabri shouted half loud. Trifko smiled at us. I sighed with relief. No more doubts; it all lay behind us.

That was a Thursday, and there was a holiday feeling about standing there on a weekday and playing hooky.

27

We steamed up the Sava for the whole day, Serbia on our port side and the Empire on our right. The ship stayed close to the Serbian shore, because the current is weaker there, a passenger told me. But if you hadn't known that, it looked as if it wanted to stay under the protection of the earth of Serbia and feared those plains under the *Kaiserlich-Koenigliche* occupation. When it got near them in a sharp bend, it seemed to speed up to get away quickly.

We saw gun emplacements on that shore, and cavalry patrols. These are an ordinary enough sight in Bosnia. Looking at them from beyond their reach, from a Serbian ship, it was different and like a challenge. I understood the gendarme who, when an Austrian gunboat passed us, pulled his revolver and cried "Bang, bang!" His colleague berated him. That gray little warship, with its eagle banner and red and green flag, did look wicked. It or one like it would one day lead the attack on Serbia; I didn't doubt it.

On both shores wheat grew, green and quite high. It had been a balmy spring. Peasants were working in the fields and staring at us from barn doors. Carts drove by, children sitting on the horses, the same skinny horses and bowlegged children on both sides of the water. On the Empire shore, the road was better, the farms poorer.

Cabri had laughed at that bang-bang of the gendarme, and the man came over to him for a chat. "You're a student going on a holiday, I bet," he began, and I heard Cabri say, "No, we're going to Bosnia, and not for a holiday either."

"To work there?" the man asked.

"To do a job, in Sarajevo," Cabri said calmly. Then, after a pause in which he ignored the frowning faces I made at him, he added, "I'm not a student, I'm a printer." That seemed to lessen his interest to the gendarme who walked away after a few more words.

Going up to Cabri, I said, "You must be out of your goddamn mind."

"I beg your pardon?" he answered.

I didn't know if he was being funny now. I surely did know that we shouldn't quarrel. There were only three of us and no one else in the world. But I said, "To talk about jobs to do in Sarajevo—how idiotic can you get?"

"Well and fuck you, too," Cabri said. "I don't need tutelage. What do you think those words could mean to him?"

"I don't know, you never know how pieces may fit together. You wanted to swear an oath so badly in Kosutnjak Park, well then, learn to keep your mouth shut."

Now Cabri was angry, too, and he walked away. Then I was sorry, of course, that I'd said that. Soon he came back, though, arm in arm with Trifko who made us shake hands. Cabri agreed that we shouldn't speak about our moves to friend or foe. He didn't stick to it, however, and later Trifko and I would get into a real fight with him on that score. Yet nobody ever had a more marvelous friend than he was.

We ate our provisions, drank water, and coffee from a bowl a peasant passed us. We read and lay on the deck, on the warm wood, with our eyes closed against the sun.

A feeling of peace and unreality.

Then the sun dipped behind a ring of black cloud, and it got cool on the water. It was early evening when the silhouette of a church tower or minaret in Sabac became distinguishable, a dark line above the misty fields.

We docked in the twilight, just as the lamp in the harbor master's office was being lit, making a yellow zigzag over the river.

28

At the Frontier Guards barracks, which faced the landing pier, a snooty corporal in the guardhouse would allow only one of us inside to look for our Sabac contact, Captain Rade. I went.

They had no electric light. I wandered across the parade ground in the rapidly falling darkness, steering toward the glimmer of a man smoking a pipe or the voices of a group talking. Shadowy faces loomed up and vanished, and no one knew where the captain was. Finally a voice from an open window called out to me, "He's likely playing cards in café

Amerika." I found my way back to the gate where Cabri and Trifko were sitting in the grass with our bundles, and told myself that I'd always expected it was going to be a mess.

I was wrong. It did work, and I later realized I had underestimated the professionalism of Milan's people. Not that that captain showed much enthusiasm to help. He looked at us from behind his hand of cards and said, "You can see I'm tied up here. But if you care to wait, I'll come and talk to you."

We picked up our bundles once more, shoved them under a table against the wall, and sat down. The café was surprisingly posh for such a small town and I was in favor of not ordering anything. But Trifko said that would make us too conspicuous, and we all had coffees. He pulled a book out of his pocket and started reading; Cabri took his pocketknife and elaborately carved an M and a C into a beer coaster. I was too weary to stir. I closed my eyes and felt the soft rolling of the riverboat in my body.

Then the captain showed up and Cabri handed him the coaster. First he was puzzled, but then he returned Cabri's smile and sat down with us.

"You boys want to cross," he said loudly.

I looked around nervously and answered, "Yes, captain."

"Yes, yes," he said and seemed lost in thought. He got out a nail file and began working on a thumb. "Klenak," he said. "Klenak village. No problems there. And it isn't more than a brisk walk from here."

"Are there no border posts in Klenak, sir?" I asked.

"Well of course there are border posts," he answered with a patient smile. "It's a border village, isn't it?"

"Oh," we said.

"Our fellows are tiptop," the captain went on, "and theirs, well, there is really only just one man, and for an Austrian he's not bad either. He plays in our euchre competition. Quite good, even. He's never given any trouble. Live and let live. Alright then?"

"Eh, well, you see, sir—" Cabri said, and I took it up, "No, that wouldn't work. We want to cross unobserved, unobserved by anyone, that is."

"Oh dammit boys," the captain answered, "You're not the first students whose papers are out of kilter. When your friends tell me to, I help them. Klenak is fine. Here's my hand on it."

He held his hand almost in my face, but though either Trifko or Cabri kicked me under the table, I didn't take it. "We don't want to trouble you, of course," I said, "but—"

"We can do some more investigating ourselves," Trifko said in a bright voice to no one in particular.

The captain dropped his hand and somberly returned to his thumbnail. There was a pause. He sighed and put away his file. "Very well," he said, "We'll do it the royal way. Someone who's a specialist. I'll give you a note for him. But he's in Loznica, two hours from here. You have money for the train, I presume."

"Oh, yes, sir," I said hastily, but now it was Cabri's turn to say, "We'd greatly appreciate it if you could give us a railway pass. We were more or less promised, in Belgrade."

The captain stood up with a pained and longing look at his card table. "Quickly then," he said. "Come to the office with me. I'll put you on our travel form for customs personnel; that'll get you half-fare. You'll still have to find yourselves a hotel for tonight, the last train is gone."

After the three of us were left in the dark street with our rail pass and our packs, and the captain had marched back to his café, I said, "Say, that went better than I had thought. He really knew that MC code."

"I bet you that VC or AD would have worked just as well," Trifko answered. "He didn't care. He just wanted to get to his cards."

"He's in training for the euchre competition with Austria," Cabri said, and we began to laugh hysterically.

"You think that Loznica contact of his is on the level?" I asked. "Maybe he was just trying to get rid of us."

Cabri shook his head. "No, he knows we'd be back and on his neck. So would Belgrade. He could see we were serious. You were very good, Gavre."

That comforted me.

We started lugging our bundles down the street and in the

next block came upon a hotel where they offered us a room with three beds for a dinar and a half.

We hid our arms in the potbellied stove and then we walked into the center of the little town and ate a gallon of beans each in a peasant inn.

29

Ask a man to help you and he may say no, or perhaps, or inquire what it's about, or then again he may immediately say yes. Our Loznica contact, who turned out to be another army captain, belonged to the last category of men. He didn't have questions. He said, "Leave it to me and it'll be arranged. Come back tomorrow at noon, ready to go." He was as simple about it as if all his days started with a request like ours. A moment later, he opened his office door again and when he saw us still standing there, he added, "Take a day off from your plans. Go to Koviljaca, that's our local resort. Very nice."

I don't know if contradictions in people like us are stronger than those in others. I know the form they take within me: I want to hope, and then I don't want to; I want to believe in humanity, and then I hate them all. And I am horrified when I am certain that it is me who is right and most everyone else who is wrong. I don't feel pride in being the only one in step. Being right and being confronted with a wrong world is a shattering experience to me. I would rather blame myself than mankind.

The Loznica captain helped me, and all three of us, by making us feel we were not that alone, out of step with everyone. He came at a crucial point, because away from Belgrade and the security of our friends, our school, our rooms, our this and that, on a boat, on a train, commercial travelers snoring behind the walls of our hotel room, we were getting slightly dizzy.

In that captain, as in Skerlic on his couch, I found a man

who without asking anything seemed to guess—to guess our state of mind, at least—and to say that we were right. But while Skerlic, sick and old, had filled me with great warmth for him, the captain gave me new spirit. We were used to having the sick and the sad side with us. A burly officer who smelled of shaving alcohol and who looked happily at the day ahead, made a rarer ally.

"Let's go to his resort," we said, "and be sightseers." We hired a room for the night first, and then boarded the steam tram that runs back and forth, at only ten cents a round trip.

The houses of Loznica were soon behind us and the track bent toward the Drina, which is the border river. Cabri poked me in my ribs as if I hadn't realized myself: there, across the water, were the green hills of Bosnia. We sat with our faces to the window, and no one said a word until the thermal bath-house of Koviljaca, grandiose with pillars and friezes, came between the river and us and cut off that view.

It was a funny place. On this weekday, and long before the summer vacations, it was as quiet as a tomb. A Grand Hotel, big as a cathedral, showed an empty lobby full of rattan chairs, with a yawning doorman in gold at the entrance. The park had a music kiosk and a drinking fountain with cups on little chains, and here a few old couples were sitting and strolling. We tried the water, which tasted bitter and muddy but in a healthy sort of way.

As we were standing around aimlessly, a man walked by under the trees at the far side, saw us, and came straight toward us. An inane chance would have it that this one other person under eighty in Koviljaca was an old friend of Cabri's. There were loud greetings and shoulder slapping, and while Trifko and I made remarks like "We must be off" and "They're waiting for us," Cabri was not to be sidetracked. He introduced us, and when his friend asked why we were there, he smiled enigmatically and pointed toward Bosnia in the distance. Who knows what he would have said if at that point Trifko hadn't literally dragged him off, leaving the friend staring slightly offended after us.

Then Trifko and Cabri had the same quarrel I had had with Cabri on the boat. And that wasn't the end of it.

Next to its spring waters, Koviljaca's main product appeared to be picture postcards, beautifully tinted photographs of the river and the town, with a straw-hatted gentleman or a lady in hoop skirts gazing at the viewer, the Drina in that special kind of postcard blue, and the roofs all cherry red. Trifko and I bought one, but Cabri bought a whole bunch. We went into a little café to eat our lunch, and I wrote my card to the friends of the Belgrade Cornerbar; I said something about being on my way to the Tromosha monastery to work in peace for my exam. We couldn't resist asking Cabri whom he was sending all his cards to, and coming on top of his quarrel with Trifko, he resented it. He read out some lines from a poem he was quoting on one of them, about a rebel during an uprising against the Turks who stares at the hills of Bosnia and thinks, "Soon the moment will come." And he had similar stuff on others, addressed to his many friends, boys and girls, from Triest to Zagreb. I grabbed a card he hadn't used yet and wrote on it, "A secret kept is your slave, a secret revealed is your master," and addressed it to him.

"You're being a schoolmaster again," Cabri said, "and you've spoiled my card."

"Well, why do you write such things?" Trifko asked.

"Because that's what's on my mind," Cabri said, "and I want my friends to know, later. Afterward. Now, no one will think anything of it."

"You're not to mail those," Trifko said, and in answer Cabri picked up his cards and walked out.

Trifko and I sat and waited, but he didn't come back. Finally we divided his congealed beans between us. We went for a walk along the Drina and we weren't in a very happy mood.

In the park, when we dropped down on a bench, Cabri reappeared and sat with us, but we didn't speak to each other the rest of the afternoon. I had brought some bread for him from the café, which he refused with a shake of his head.

There didn't seem to be anything else to do but to go back

to the terminal and wait for a streetcar back to Loznica. We were the only passengers. It was Cabri who broke the silence.

"Sorry, fellows," he said, "but I think being natural is our best protection. I'm not going to act out Rinaldo Rinaldini, or The Beautiful Spy for the Czar."

I couldn't help laughing, but Trifko refused to be amused. "I'm not going on with you," he said, "You're a fine man, but you're not my choice to sneak across a frontier with. We'll meet up in Tuzla."

Cabri and I looked at each other. Trifko was hard to budge when he had decided something. I thought he was probably right, anyway. Tuzla, thirty miles beyond the border, is the first real town in Bosnia, and we all knew it; we had all gone to grade school there at one time.

Trifko pulled out his school registration card. "It's really better," he told Cabri. "You take my card and cross openly. A division of risks."

"And what about my weapons?" Cabri asked.

"Let Gavre and me carry them for you. You take them back from us when we're across, in Tuzla."

Cabri now began to look crestfallen and hurt. Still, I didn't want to be a weakling and when he turned to me, I said, "I do agree with Trifko. No aspersion on you. You don't have the temperament for dissimulation—for lying."

Cabri shrugged and accepted Trifko's school card. "I'll abide by the majority decision," he said slowly. "I'll leave today. See you in Tuzla. In our old café."

30

Our magic walk.

Trifko and I walked four days, or, better, nights (for we usually waited until dark)—from that captain's office in Loznica to close to Tuzla, sleeping once at an army post, once on an uninhabited island in the Drina, and once in a peasant hut, each carrying three hand grenades, two pistols, and thirty rounds of ammunition. Trifko had our spare clothes crammed in his pockets, for I was, insanely, also carrying my books, two dozen of them, which I refused to leave behind or just drop, although the temptation to do that was enormous. I should, of course, have given them to Cabri to take. We walked through woods and a swamp and freshly plowed fields and through the Drina River; and in the night of June 1 through the most violent mountain storm I'd ever seen. We never saw a trace of an Austrian soldier or gendarme.

I had never before been so tired, so wet and muddy and hungry. But we called it our magic walk. We were in a high state, hard to put into words, a state of excitement or, at times, of exaltation even.

Why, I don't completely know.

For one thing, we weren't marking time any more, this was it; but we were blissfully freed from those bloodcurdling confrontations with "normalcy" and "normal people." And Sarajevo and June 28 were still far in the future.

It was a green walk. The vast, friendly forests of our Bosnia were all around us and over us. Trees, bushes, leaves, grass, and even the water we waded through was green, was ours, and the slashing rain was green, and not inimical. I saw us as if from an imaginary height, two tiny figures moving along this huge earth, protected by that early summer canopy of nature. Can you imagine being too weary to take another step and at the same time feeling intensely and superiorly alive? I was aware of every inch of my body and I talked to my feet and hands like a sergeant to his wayworn but loyal platoon. I felt the wet weight of those hand grenades against my skin, and it was the proper feeling. All was well. When one of us let a branch jump back too soon and it hit the other in his face, we laughed.

For we liked those wet leaves in our faces. They were our leaves.

How do I know Trifko felt like that? When I said, during the third night, "This is a magic walk," he wasn't surprised but quickly answered, "Yes, I know." At that moment we were stumbling over the hard furrows in a dark and sloping and endless field. And when we got to a hut before dawn and sat together, taking off our shoes and our grenades, he said, "It's like being medieval knights."

"Knights on foot."

Trifko thought about that and answered, "That's the good part of it! We aren't like men who've lost something, who have to make do without horses, we've gone beyond that, this is such an intense charge that we had to keep our feet on the ground, not to fly away, that's why we have to walk toward Sarajevo—" Then he laughed shyly and said, "Oh, I don't know. Let's sleep."

There's a mood I've named for myself the splinter-of-time awareness. It rarely comes over me, and till then only when in a depression of hopelessness.

I want to explain what it means.

The first time I thought of it in that particular way was in school, our Latin professor describing the Roman games in the Colosseum.

I faced an amphitheater packed with men and women in the bright sunlight, and I was to die. They looked at me without seeing me, seeing only a nude animated body about to be ripped open for them, to give them a sensual shiver of pleasure. Then, standing there, I thought, this is only a splinter of time, a sliver within eons. They and I will all die at the same moment.

But I got no courage from that, for my splinter of time, in the sun, my naked feet on the sand of the arena, was totally the present, the center of time and space. It overwhelmed everything else, oceans and stars, and nothing else mattered but the unique sequence of events that had brought me there, a Serbian captive, and would let me die there.

It may all sound very confused.

The walk through the woods with Trifko was such a splinter of time. Nothing else existed or mattered. And within that present we were magically happy.

31

The logistics of our walk had a clockwork precision. At the captain's office, we had met a frontier-post sergeant, an enormous fellow with a face like a Montenegrin mountainside. "You'll cross at his post," the captain said, gave us a hard look, and wished us luck.

The sergeant set us on a quick march through the Loznica Saturday market crowd and out into the woods in a flash, Trifko and I half walking, half trotting after him. "Why are we going north?" we asked. "Because that's where my post it. What's all that stuff under your jackets? You want me to carry some of it? I won't mind." We looked at each other and regretfully declined. Those hand grenades weighed more than three pounds each and were the devil to keep in place.

It must have been a full fifteen miles to his post. We slept there. The following morning he took us still farther north and then in a rowboat to Isakovico, a little island in the Drina, Serbian territory and without inhabitants. He marched (he was unable to walk at a normal pace, Trifko and I agreed) through the willow groves covering it; we came out at the other side, and there we found a little café. Our sergeant winked heavily, enjoyed our surprise, and waited for us to laugh. The café was for selling brandy on the sly to the peasants of Bosnia who didn't mind crossing a ford in the river to get a good, untaxed drink. He wasn't doing this for his own profit but secretly-officially, to have a contact post with Bosnians. Or that's how he told it to us.

We sat around that long Sunday. No one came for the cheap brandy. In the late afternoon a peasant arrived, a man of fifty or more, with a kind, weatherbeaten look. He was our passeur, the sergeant said, the name they give men who make it their business to know their way around army posts and patrols. The passeur had a shot of brandy, we had a glass of black coffee, and off went the three of us through the icy river and up the shore.

Bosnia.

The passeur stopped, unbuttoned his trousers, and pissed against the first tree while looking at us. We sort of smiled, but he shook his head gravely. "Do the same," he said, "it's for good luck, it's a tried way to stay clear of the Austrians." And it was.

This gentle old man walked with hardly a rest from ten that night until seven the following evening, through a thunderstorm, up and down rocky hills, through woods and brooks and sand. Trifko and I stumbled-floated behind him, in the state I've described. When we sat down, unable to move, he told us cheerfully, "Ten more minutes." Up we got, and after precisely ten minutes we found ourselves at a hut where a woodcutter gave us coffee and goat's cheese.

The next evening we came to a village called Priboj. Here our passeur brought out a melancholy-looking man with a long mustache whose name was Veljiko and who was a teacher. He didn't ask questions either and took us for granted; when he saw what state we were in, he went to get a sack and said, "Put your things in here." As he seemed to know or guess it all, we simply brought out our arms and did as he asked. The passeur had disappeared in the meantime, but in his place another peasant showed up, and now we all took turns carrying our load.

We walked and walked in a half dream. The rain had stopped and a thin moon was shining falsely between the clouds. We went over farm land now and the earth was as slippery as ice. It must have been the dead middle of the night when we came to yet another hut. Veljiko the teacher said it was safe for us to sleep there. He gave some money to the peasant and told him sternly to keep his mouth shut, or else. We added a crown, and a similar warning about "vengeance from Belgrade" if he didn't. This was for his own protection, of course; his defense, that he had been forced to help us, later saved his life.

The owner of the hut was an old peasant named Mitar. He

poured us glasses of plum brandy, and then Trifko and I lay down on a blanket on the floor and slept like the dead. Before dawn, Mitar shook us awake and put us and our stuff on his horse cart, and off we went, chop-chop, to Tuzla. It was superb luxury to sit, legs stretched out, and be driven, to watch the trees go by and look up at the sky without moving a muscle.

A mile before Tuzla we got off. Mitar went on to leave the sack with another contact, whom we would meet later. I wanted to take out my books first, but he said I might as well keep them in with the rest. The sun was out, and Trifko and I washed our mud-caked clothes in the stream running along the road. We shook and wrung every piece as hard as possible, put it back on and jumped up and down to get warm and dry. "We still look like hell," Trifko said, inspecting me, "your trousers are all torn, your ass is sticking out." His was, too.

In the town, we went to the general store at the first cross-roads and bought ourselves a pair of work pants each, and a pocket comb, and threw our old trousers away. We walked into Tuzla and no one stared at us.

32

Our Tuzla rendezvous was the local Serbian reading room, a church-supported institution where bloodless Serbian pub-lications were made available, in heavy wooden holders to make sure no one would steal the damn things. Here a lean, elegant gentleman was sitting, the contact Mitar had de-scribed to us, one of the prominent citizens of Tuzla, member of the board of directors of the Serbian Bank, owner of the first movie house in town.

Yet he was an enemy of that Empire that would have engaged its army and navy if necessary to protect his wealth and prop-erty. We knew only his first name then, Misko.

We sat across from him, picked up magazines to give us a pose, and I asked him, "Did someone bring you our things, sir?"

"Yes," he said, "they're in a box now."

"Would you be able to take them into Sarajevo one day?"

He hesitated.

"My friend and I here used to be under police surveillance," I added, "and maybe we still are."

"Do you go to Sarajevo occasionally?" Trifko asked.

"Yes, I do," he answered but said no more.

"It's partly books," Trifko said idiotically.

"Perhaps this is the best way," I suggested, "if you'd be willing to take the risk of keeping the box for a few days, either I or a friend will come and pick it up."

"How will I be sure he's a friend?" Misko asked.

"He'll give a password," Trifko said. "I know, he'll offer you a Stefanija cigarette."

Misko smiled at that. "All right," he muttered, and left hastily. But he turned out to be a very brave man.

Trifko and I waited a minute or two after him and then, sore-legged as we were, almost ran to our old Tuzla café hangout. There he was at the window, as groomed as a cat—our Cabri. "Jesus, you boys look terrible," was the first thing he said. "You—you look beautiful," Trifko shouted. We were crazily happy to see each other. Each of us said that from now on, no matter what, we'd stick together.

"They say the police are checking all the roads into Sarajevo, and the railway station too," Cabri said.

"They always do."

"Much more systematically now. And you can be sure it'll get worse as that Visit approaches."

"We'll go on today," I said. "I know there is an afternoon train."

"And our stuff?" he asked.

"It's safe for the moment, here in Tuzla. It was quite a haul; you don't know what you missed."

Cabri's face clouded over. "I can imagine from looking at you two," he said. "And I wonder how I can make up for it. I'm in your debt now."

"No," Trifko and I cried simultaneously. "Not at all," I said. "You missed something marvelous."

He looked at us in surprise and we tried to explain to him,

interrupting each other, in half sentences, that we had never been as happy as when we slugged through the mud of Bosnia's borderland with those weapons. He didn't understand or he wouldn't believe us; he thought we were just trying to make him feel better.

That afternoon we took the train to Sarajevo.

33

Bosna Serai, the castle of Bosnia, that was Sarajevo's name in the time of the Turks. We wanted to restore that fame to it.

It's odd how the Turkish days in all their horror now look less uniformly black than the days of Austria. At times the Turks had shown a certain grandiosity; inefficiency had mitigated their greed. The Austrian occupation would never be anything else but a nightmare: modern cruelty is harder than primitive cruelty. It is less deadening to be suppressed by warriors than by sadistic grocers and clerks set loose far from home.

I have been told that the earliest memory of childhood that you retain is an important clue to your character. I don't know what mine means and I am not even sure it is real and not a dreamed remembrance from a picture in a book. But it is of myself as a small child walking along Sarajevo's river, the Miljacka, at my mother's hand.

That river used to meander through the town, within its bends flat sandy banks where children played. Orchards and decorative gardens lined the river, one after the other—for the Turks had brought the pleasure gardens of Persia into the Balkans (as the Arabs brought them into Spain). Later the river was canalized by the Austrians between stone banks, and behind a wall as if it were something that shouldn't be seen. They built a quay where the gardens had been and named it after a baron of theirs called Appel. They replaced the narrow footbridge with what is now called the Latin Bridge. Sarajevo was occupied by the Habsburg army in the summer of 1878, sixteen years before I was born; I've never asked my mother if she once brought me to Sarajevo as a baby.

But in that earliest memory there is no wall and no quay. My mother and I cross the footbridge over the Miljacka and walk along the water, under the fruit trees. On her free arm hangs a large basket. The air is sweet and warm and the sun dapples the grass under the foliage.

Up on the hillside looms an ugly gray hunk of stone. That would be the Francis Joseph barracks, and it's still there. But we turn our backs on it. My mother takes off my sandals and lets me shuffle and run through the grass and the sand.

At one point, I suddenly realize I am alone and I freeze and turn around.

She is standing under a tree, in the sunlight, and smiles at me. I run toward her. I ache with love for her.

34

As Trifko, Cabri, and I got off the train in Sarajevo and walked along the platform under the steam-filled glass dome that echoed voices and the hissing of the engine, a different time clock started up. I repeated to myself, twenty-three. Twenty-three. There were, or I had, twenty-three days left. Trifko saw my lips move and asked, "What?" "Nothing." Police were checking luggage and parcels at the exit gate. We walked past them without looking in their faces.

It was still daylight out and the sky, without the intercession of grimy train windows, was a startlingly bright lime green. Shouts rose from men drilling in the military manège across the road. *Im Arbeitstempo, trab! Im Galopp, marsch!* We couldn't see them, but the feathers on the helmet of one of the riders stuck out over the wall, bouncing by as if a bird were fluttering there, Trifko said. "More like someone jogging around on the other side with a severed head on a pole," Cabri answered. We stood still.

"It's his cavalry escort already preparing."

"Oh, who knows."

"I'm going on to Pale," Trifko said. "I'm best off staying with my parents. They won't be too surprised, they always trust me." We asked him how he'd get there, for it is way out in the country. There was a little local train from the Mariendvor terminal. "I'll be back in, tomorrow or the day after," he said. Handshakes.

"And you?" Cabri asked. "And you?" I asked back. He was going to stay with his parents, too. "I won't get into any arguments with my father," he said. "I'll tell him I have come back for a better job in a printing house here. He won't ask me anything else."

As for me, I went back to my old boardinghouse, where I had lived when I went to school in Sarajevo and where the son of the landlady had become my friend, though he was four years older than I. I had brooded about that move. It was the only place where I'd be let in without first registering with the police, and it was the logical choice. Everyone would expect me to stay there again. But it could create a risk for my friend, Danilo.

Of course it was a grave error that I did go back. We weren't political plotters; we were actors in a morality play. Or so we felt.

Danilo was away. His mother welcomed me without any fuss; she assumed my school had accepted me again. There were only a few boarders and she gave me my old room. It was fourteen crowns a month. I paid ten and promised her the remaining four the following week.

I was sitting at my old window, looking out over Oprkanj Street as if nothing had happened. I had to fight off a great somberness when I thought how I'd left that room half a year before, not expecting to see it ever again. That passed. I wasn't sitting there like a high school boy any more.

But I had no courage just then to go into town and meet friends from that bygone past. I had no courage to see Sophia. It was a soft summer evening and I was very cold. I closed the window, took off my shoes, and crept under the cover with all my clothes on.

35

I walked through the Turkish bazaar and looked at the leather-work and the carpets as if I were a tourist from London or Vienna; I sat at a little table and asked for unsweetened coffee. That morning I was a stranger in Sarajevo, a very lonely traveler. I was carrying the Andreyev book, but without looking them up I remembered those words Trifko had read to me one night, "a haze, peculiar to persons carried away by some all-absorbing great idea." I felt no such haze enveloping me.

To the contrary, I saw and heard everything with a cutting precision: the roof edges, the hilltops, the plum trees, in which a few dried-out blossoms still clung, stood out so sharply against the sky, the sounds of the life around me were so ringingly clear, as if this were taking place in a vast, dry Sahara desert. Was it not a great idea, then, that had brought us here? I told myself that I had without doubt taken one more step up that imaginary stairway.

Near twelve o'clock I walked over to Sophia's school and waited across the road. When school got out, she was one of the first to appear and in one movement saw me, turned to me, and began crossing the road. She stood still in front of me and stared at me without surprise or hesitation.

I half smiled.

"How pale you are," she said softly.

"Oh—" I began and didn't know what else to say.

She pulled my head down with both her hands and touched my forehead with her lips. Then she took my hand and walked on quickly, making me stay beside her. I saw a tear run down her cheek, saw her brush it away with her sleeve, and did not say anything about it.

She never asked why I was back.

We walked north and up the hillside, sat down on a bench

and looked out over the lilac bushes and the faded red roofs and domes and minarets. We could see the river, and a cloud of steam and smoke from a train. After a while I said, "Don't make yourself late for afternoon school." She shook her head and answered, "It doesn't matter."

She played with the fingers of my hand, and then said, "Read me something from your book."

I opened it at several places, but the words all stuck in my throat. She took it out of my hands and leafed through it; finally she stopped at a page and started reading very clearly.

"What do those people think? That there is nothing more terrible than death. They themselves have invented Death, they themselves are afraid of it, and they try to frighten us with it.

"When thousands kill one, it means that the one has won."

Her voice trailed off. "Is that true?" she asked.

"Yes, I think so."

"Is that why you're not afraid of death?" Her voice was light.

"How do you know I'm not?" I asked and smiled at her. At that moment, for the first time, I saw her again. Saw her sea eyes and that soft round line of her dress, the black stockings hiding her legs, fifteen-year-old girl's legs.

"I just know," she said. "I'm not afraid either. But you must answer my question."

I thought about it. "My parents had nine children," I answered, "Nine in all, that is. Three of us are alive. Some died before me, but I remember two sisters dying; they were only two or three years old. The priest did come, but he looked a bit distracted. The death of young children on the mountain farms of Bosnia is no great event. But you know all that."

"Yes . . ." she said, and waited for more.

"That is your answer," I said. "The spark struck—"

"The spark?" In a high voice.

"I don't mean to sound like a German poet," I said. "I just now thought of it that way. Sparks struck in a woman's womb. In my mother's womb. Most of them die out before there is even a small flame. A game of chance, and such overwhelming odds against one, any one, single, never seen or repeated, life."

She pursed her mouth and sighed.

I began to laugh. "Oh, Sophia," I said, "Vukosava Sophia . . . did I disappoint you?"

"Yes."

"I know. You had expected an inspired statement on personal sacrifice and the future of the people."

"Yes."

"Don't you know those statements are made only by elderly statesmen, who've just come back from a visit to their physician who's measured their blood pressure and smelled their —looked at their tongue and told them to cut down from twenty to five Havana cigars?"

She looked down on the page in Andreyev. "Are those the people 'who invented Death'?" she asked.

I didn't know what to answer to that. Now it seemed highly mysterious to me that some gentleman in Vienna who gave worried thought to the yes or no of his sixth cigar and who felt his own pulse before going to sleep, could so easily discuss war and peace, prisons and the scaffold.

"Perhaps it's their appetite," Sophia said. "I mean animals, who are innocent, of course, just eat when they're hungry. It's all they know. A bird eats a worm and can't think if the worm is suffering. It's hungry and that's all. Perhaps those old men who eat up Bosnia are too hungry to know anything else."

"Sophia . . . ?" I asked after a while.

"Yes?"

"When will you be sixteen?"

"In September. Only three months."

Only three months.

She held the book out for me to take back. I used the movement to touch her with the palm of my hand, to touch her breast very lightly.

36

In the night the creaking floor of the landing woke me up. I looked around my door and saw Danilo about to go into his room. He came and sat in my window sill and I crept back into bed. Through the open curtain, moonlight flooded the room. We used to have night talks that way in the past, with the light off, for if we turned it on, his mother would mysteriously wake up and come to complain about the electricity bill.

Danilo, an ex-schoolteacher, ex-all kinds of jobs, twenty-two or twenty-three years old, was at that time a proofreader. I knew he was wiser than most authors whose work he had to proof, but he was too restless and unorthodox to write himself, except for pieces in our illegal or half-legal publications. I had learned very much from him during my years in that boardinghouse. Even when I was thirteen and he seventeen, he had never been patronizing with me.

"So you're already here for Vidovdan," were his first words, after he had installed himself and lit a cigarette. He didn't ask; he registered the fact. I couldn't answer in any way but with "Yes."

"Saint Vitus Day," Danilo said. (That's what Vidovdan means, of course). "Isn't it just like us Slavs to have our great national commemoration on the day of Saint Vitus. There's the perfect saint for us."

"The saint of madmen."

"I know all about him; I proofread an essay on the subject by some damn professor, he's not only the patron of madmen but also of epileptics, wine growers, actors, soldiers (infantry, that is, of course), dumb people, deaf people, landlords of inns, men struck by lightning or bitten by snakes, there's more—wait—children who pee in bed and girls who defend their chastity. He's usually shown with a crow, and he was murdered by our own local prodigy, Emperor Diocletian."

He had trouble with his cigarette, threw it out of the window, and rolled a new one.

In the silence, the bells of a church nearby struck two o'clock.

"Do you have weapons?" Danilo asked.

"Yes."

A new pause. I realized he wasn't going to ask more. "They're not here yet," I told him. "They're in Tuzla. I have to go get them, but I'm not sure yet how."

"I'll do it."

"No."

"Yes."

"I've no right to let someone else run that risk," I said.

He shrugged. I couldn't see it but I guessed, from the sound of his jacket rubbing against the wood of the window. "You've no right to risk it yourself. If they catch someone else, you can try again, through another channel. That's the ABC of action. I taught you that," he ended with a little laugh.

"Aren't you under surveillance?"

"No longer. I've been clear for two years now. And I proof-read all sorts of government crap. They assume I've learned the facts of life by now. Besides, I know how to go about a thing like that."

"How?"

He was taking a sharp pull on his cigarette; I saw it glow. You could tell he enjoyed explaining this. "Tuzla—" he said. "Right. In that case, whatever you want to smuggle in, you get off with it at Alipasa Bridge. There's nothing at that stop, no police ever. At Alipasa, you take the local train to Ilidza. But you don't stay on till Ilidza. That train, for obscure reasons, has a stop at Mariendvor. Never a soul there. No control either. At Mariendvor you get off and you have a streetcar to get home." He chuckled. "The mighty empires of the wicked all have their little forgotten Mariendvors. Though, one day, they may learn to bar those, too. Then we've had it."

"One day. Unless we win first."

"You know, Gavre," he said, "I don't believe in what you are doing. The timing is wrong for violent deeds."

That stopped me dead. "Then I surely don't want you to go to Tuzla. That'd be doubly insane, to take a risk like that for something you don't believe in."

"But I believe in friendship," Danilo said. "That's what it's all about, isn't it? Or, if you don't mind pathos, brotherhood."

"I must also get you a suit," Danilo continued, taking my work pants off a chair and holding them near the window to see better. "These won't do. A suit, a shirt with a white collar, and a tie. Look like a clerk. Where are your own clothes?"

"My suit is at my brother's place. I'm not sure I want to go there."

"Don't. I can get hold of one that'll fit. Now I'd better go to bed and let us both get some sleep."

"I want to tell you a story first," I said. "I read it this afternoon, I was sitting in the town library. It's in the travel memoirs of Humboldt. He's in Paramaribo—you know where that is?"

"I forget. South America."

"Yes. A Dutch colony. The burgomaster or someone invited him to visit the new hospital, they were so proud of it. Then, in a waiting room, Humboldt came upon two Negro slaves, huge fellows sitting there quietly, with a soldier between them. They were shackled. 'What are they here for?' Humboldt asked. 'For an operation,' an attendant told him. 'An operation? They look very fine and healthy to me.' 'They're runaway slaves, caught two days ago.' 'And?' 'They get their left leg cut off.' Humboldt thought the man was joking. 'It's the law,' they told him very gravely, 'but it's done by the surgeon. We're no barbarians.' He fled from that place in horror. Imagine the doctor coming in and asking with a little smile, 'Who'll be first?' Isn't that a terrifying story, more terrifying than any history of a massacre?"

"Why did you tell it to me?" Danilo asked.

"I don't want to sit in Bosnia, waiting, like those slaves."

"The comparison hobbles, Gavrilo," he told me.

"It's a parable. Our century cripples men."

I left the curtain open after he had gone and could see the moon now from my bed. I tried to think what arguments I ought to have used with Danilo, but I felt myself gliding into a dream.

I know dreams are symbolic, not literal, but that night and often afterward I dreamed simply of the Sarajevo police chasing me. Those weren't nightmares; I had a good time; they didn't catch me.

37

Three days later the Tuzla box of arms, and books, was under my bed when I came home. I cleaned the pistols as Milan had shown me and wrapped the grenades in a blanket with great care. I looked a while in silence at that bottle with cloudy liquid that was labeled "Danger": prussic acid, hydrocyanide, HCN. Not quite comprehensible that those three simple parts of nature, hydrogen, carbon, nitrogen, should together become like a chemical scorpion, devouring your blood in one bite. It was better not to think about it if possible.

I got together with Trifko and Cabri to give them their stuff. They took only a pistol and a grenade each, and poison. We agreed that we mustn't be seen too much in each other's company. We shouldn't avoid other students: there was bound to be all kinds of police checking and observing people going on, with the visit creeping nearer.

A different frame of mind from our happy reunion in Tuzla, where we'd said we'd stick together from then on—it was the shade cast by that bottle of acid. "But we are sticking together where it counts," Cabri said, "whether we see each other or not."

Cabri took a job, which seemed an amazing show of self-discipline to me until I followed his example a week later and found it easier than I had thought. Mine was copying the minutes of the Prosvjeta, a Serb welfare organization. I paid my debts with the money. As for Trifko, he stayed with his parents in Pale most days. He had his girl friend there, too, a very gay young teacher at the Pale grade school. I don't know what he told her.

The Sarajevo evenings were toughest, it stayed light so long, an uncertain golden light caught between the houses that filled me with melancholy touches of fear, a near morbid impatience.

I usually went to the Semiz café then, a nicely normal activity in case the police were watching. It was a place where they served only wine and where I'd never set foot before. Now I wanted to be seen with the kind of people who had made it their hangout. I knew one of them, a student called Jevtic, and he took me in with a lot of warmth. Those boys were all for and against the proper things, but they were just messing around; they were bohemians, they said. What meaning could it have, their artistic withdrawal from the order established over us? The owner of the Semiz made some money, while the Empire surely didn't give a damn. There are only two sides to a barricade. But I kept my mouth shut.

The mayor, or whoever does those things, picked on the name of the street that the Semiz café was on, in his program of festivities. A long-dead Hungarian general bit the dust and had to give way to the satrap, and there we were on Francis Ferdinand Street! I decided to consider it a good omen. Why not.

The students made endless jokes about it. Two boys insisted on treating everyone for the occasion and proposed all sorts of crazy toasts. But they went on and on about who could hold his wine best. One of them kept pushing a glass against my lips, telling me not to be afraid, until I was so mad that I got up to hit him. He backed away and I was ashamed. "Don't be such a slob," I said lamely.

"Don't you be so contemptuous, Gavre," Jevtic answered for him. "Everyone must get drunk at times."

"That's fine with me," I said. "Only don't ask me to share your tender interest in your own cosy bodily functions. We've got more serious enemies to hold out against than O-H groups."

That created great hilarity at our table. "O-H groups?" they repeated. I began to laugh, too. "I took chemistry in Belgrade," I said, "look it up." And they kept saying, "O-H groups! Who wants another glass of O-H groups?"

I stood outside. Just one single star was visible that night in an ink-black sky. I walked under a mystery, for there were large clouds flying across and yet whenever I looked up, that one star was there. I liked the taste of wine in my mouth, which I hadn't known before, but it had no effect on me. If being drunk is, as Jevtic told me, being freed of yourself, I was getting drunk along a different road. My anti-private-life battle.

I walked through Sophia's street and as I passed her house, I shouted against the wind, "Sophia!" without stopping. In my room, I opened the window. I wasn't cold any more now, never. I let the curtain wave and flutter, I kept looking at the star, I let unformed thoughts chase through my mind. I brought Sophia into my river orchards child memory of Sarajevo. She lay in the grass, sometimes in her school dress, sometimes naked. Then I didn't dare look at her belly, for I wasn't sure how a girl's belly is shaped and I didn't want the image to shatter. I thought, let me see it as a y, a flowery y. I had leaves and shades glide over her skin. In-ness, drowning.

The black night wind traveling over the town.

Insects flew in, at my face, night moths. I had to duck for them, and they couldn't find their way back out. I took one that was miserably fluttering in a corner by its wing to get it to the window, and then it suddenly seemed a prehistoric weird thing and I let go of it with some fear.

Danilo's voice. A man had come to see him, with a message for me and "my associates." "He must have gotten to me through my Tuzla expedition," Danilo said. "They don't seem very careful to me, those people. I told him that I knew nothing about your plans and wasn't aware of who 'your associates' might be. Then he insisted on making me the recipient of the message."

The message was of a supposed change of heart of Milan's Belgrade friends, identified as "MC." They were now sorry they had provided us with what the man had called, tools, and they asked us to reconsider. They felt this wasn't the time for adventurism. Danilo, of course, happened to agree with that, but he had asked the emissary sternly, "Why not?" Because there was no political organization to profit from it, and because of retaliation against innocent people.

"Did you cry, 'There are no innocents!'" I asked Danilo.

He smiled. "Have you considered that you and we all are perhaps just being used?"

"Cabri would answer, 'So what?' It's the perfect answer. We are no dupes; no one talked us into anything. I don't care what some crooked politician may want to make of us. Their words and even their deeds have no bearing on our reality."

"All right," he said. "Now here's a worse possibility. Suppose you and I and we all just make our own people uncomfortable? Just *bore* the world?"

"You don't get me with that either. No big shock. I don't overestimate human wickedness. A victim must often do nothing so much as bore his executioner. And himself. I bore myself with my own crappy righteousness."

"But you're happy with that?"

"Oh, damn you," I said, "I didn't want to hold forth like this. If I'm not happy, I'm happy being unhappy. You know, nothing is more satisfactory than the happiness of others. It doesn't turn sour, you can go on believing in it."

"You fellows think in crucial deeds and crucial dates," Danilo answered, "but the crucial dates in history are a secret until long after." He opened my door, for he has a habit of walking out after making a statement like that; I jumped up and caught him by his sleeve.

"Not always!" I shouted.

"Hey, I almost forgot," Danilo said from the landing. "I have use for the weapons left over."

"But—" I began.

"Perhaps you've convinced me." This time he vanished before I could say more.

38

Ilidza is a little resort town half an hour to the south of us, up toward the mountains, with phosphate springs to cure, I'm not sure what, overeating maybe. Here, the papers informed us, would be the archducal headquarters for the army maneuvers and the Sarajevo visit.

A good idea to have a look around there. I went with Trifko, who brought his girl friend to make it more natural and innocent, while Cabri would go reconnoiter on another day, and with his mother in tow.

Trifko and the girl met me at the station. Her name was

Leposava, and she looked just as happy as I'd last remembered her, a year ago. We set out for the Bosna Hotel. She fell behind when we passed some market booths, and Trifko asked me in an undertone, "Have you heard about the schools?" "No, what?" "All schools are to close early this year, and students who don't live in Sarajevo will have to leave town right away." Leposava caught up with us before I could answer. We'll have to register at our Sarajevo addresses, I thought.

The Bosna Hotel was in an uproar of carpenters, painters, and masons, with ladders and plaster everywhere. Men were lugging chairs and carpets, and the sound of hammering reverberated through the lobby. I walked over to the desk of the concierge (I was wearing that suit and white collar Danilo had provided) and asked, "Where can we have tea?" On the terrace in the garden, the concierge said; everything else was temporarily closed. "We're being entirely refurbished," he added.

"Refurbished? For the visit of His Highness?" I asked.

"For the visit of His Imperial and Royal Highness. The entire hotel will be taken over. Let me show you something."

He came out from behind his desk and guided us through the lobby and into what must have been the writing room. They were just carrying out a last writing table. A battery of workmen on ladders were in the process of covering the walls with gold cloth, on which black Austrian double-headed eagles and crucifixes alternated. The walls, in white and green, had had bucolic scenes in which shepherdesses were crowning each other and bunches of naked babies with wreaths of flowers, and it was a strange spectacle to see them all gradually disappear under the gold and black cloth. Against the back wall, two men were raising a gilded Christ with ropes and pulleys that came down from a little balcony.

"Forty thousand gold crowns," the concierge said with satisfaction. "That's what it'll cost."

"My," Leposava sighed.

"Just for this chapel, mind you," he told us.

"But why?" Trifko asked. "What is it for?", keeping his voice full of awe, however.

"Their Highnesses always insist on a mass in private," the concierge announced.

"Their Highnesses?"

"The Duchess will be here, too."

"More bad news," Trifko murmured in my ear.

"Gentlemen, young lady," the concierge said, and opening another door, led us through a corridor and out into a garden.

"What's here?" Trifko asked.

"For your tea," the concierge said. "Down that path, if you please." And he disappeared with a little bow.

Trifko and Leposava began to laugh. "We're not going to have tea here," she said, "there'll be ladies in big hats staring at me, and it'll cost a fortune."

"And there'll be a string quartet squeaking away," Trifko said.

"Oh, let's," I asked them.

"Why?"

"I don't know."

There was nothing to reconnoiter in the tea garden, which doubtlessly would be closed once the satrap arrived. To be precise, I was trying not even to think of him just then. I wanted to sit in that sunny garden and sip tea, next to the ladies in the big hats and the string orchestra; I wanted to have done that once. If only to despise it.

But there were no ladies and no violinists. The three of us were the first guests, and we were seated at a balustrade above a pond with two swans. They brought us tea, and Leposava poured it. The singing of the birds in the circle of trees won out over the sound of hammering from the hotel. A bee fell in the milk but was saved by Trifko. The air was warm and smelled of the grass and the flowers.

Trifko's girl whispered something to him.

The clear note of a teacup hitting its saucer.

I felt a bodily pain grip me, pain about the world that was or appeared so beautiful, so large, and so overflowing with a myriad possibilities. This Bosnian garden, and beyond it were soundless mountains, pampas, jungle rivers, lights going on in faraway cities at the sea.

Would we really have the courage to turn our backs on everything?

Suppose it were all canceled; suppose that fucking archduke stayed in Vienna, or that we'd just say to each other, "Oh, to hell with it!" It would be like a concrete wall opening or turning into glass, a sunny panorama of limitless width suddenly at our feet.

Leposava stood up and went to feed a biscuit to the swans.

I turned to Trifko. "About that school closing. We must register at Sarajevo addresses, quickly."

"Yes, I've thought of that," Trifko answered. "You and Cabri will be all right where you are. I'll have a problem."

He shook me gently by my shoulder. "Don't look so worried," he said. "I'll manage something."

I pressed my lips together and nodded.

39

Back in Sarajevo, I didn't go home but walked to the Kosovo Cemetery.

I sat on the stone of Zerajic's blank grave. As usual, the flowers had gone: every day visitors put them there and every day the caretaker, under police orders, took them away again. An interesting Empire, which saw to such details.

I stood up to take some flowers from elsewhere, as I used to do with Sophia, but then I sat down again.

I was perfectly aware that that particular spot was in no way different or closer to Zerajic than any other spot in the world, that death means disappearance, that there are no "remains." The thought that his friends would come to this place might have helped Zerajic while he was still alive, but whether they actually did, once he was dead, made no earthly difference.

How to explain to myself what I was doing there?

I guessed it was more or less that business again of our oath in Kosutnjak Park; I was fighting to get back in that mood.

I thought I needed all the help I could get, and this setting was a help.

Kosovo Cemetery, named after our fatal Kosovo battlefield, the Field of the Crows. Vitus Day. Turks. Austrians. June 28. Fatally, capriciously, it all did fit together.

But how easy it must have been for our Kosovo folk hero Milos Obilic to kill the wicked Sultan of the Turks, and how hard for Zerajic five hundred years later to fire on General Varesanin. Zerajic, like every schoolchild, had been told ad infinitum about those medieval people's heroisms, and like every schoolchild he had been turned, individualized, against them.

I felt I was getting hold of an important thread of truth there.

The wind blew a flurry of dead leaves into my lap. I looked around. Not a soul. It was darkening; the lonely light at the cemetery gate was already on. Steps on the gravel where some late visitor was leaving—who would come here at this hour, on a weekday? I put my hand down flat beside me on the rough stone, and imagined talking with Zerajic.

Something like this: school education, his kind and my kind, was supposed to mean learning all about the thoughts of Caesar or Newton or Pascal, becoming aware of your own uniqueness and intellectual nobility, and so on and on. But the men who had thought those thoughts had been masters of the world. Even those who, as it was always put in our schoolbooks, were "of humble origin." Those, too, had accepted the ways of power of the world. At least sufficiently to survive. And with that, they, like we, had learned contempt, suspicion, or irony for common feeling and common action. Common itself had come to mean vulgar, and vulgar no longer meant, of the people, but: vulgar. The individual, in a perfect contradiction, was all.

But neither Zerajic nor I was, or wanted to be, master of the world.

We didn't wish to be anyone's, not even our own, blind followers. But neither did we wish, though it had been drilled into us that we should wish it, to stand out on top of a pile of others.

We were not political Young Werthers, tearfully involved in private heroics.

The only way to be a twentieth-century Milos Obilic was to strip yourself of all that, to act from the commonalty. Because otherwise the battle will be nothing but a never-ending change of generals and it will never be over.

Too ingenuous, maybe. Our professors yawn. It worked for me. It had worked for Zerajic. We knew what it meant.

To hell with the Ilidza tea garden.

It was completely dark now. The wind was rustling through the trees, traveling up the paths of the cemetery, as if people were softly hurrying off in all directions.

In spite of my reasoning, I sat there with tears in my eyes, tears for Zerajic who had carried a piece of cardboard, with the picture of a boy holding a red flag, on his heart when he shot himself and died on the Emperor Bridge. Our police had imagined it was a secret badge and had sent reproductions of it to their colleagues in all the capitals of Europe. But it was just the cover of Kropotkin's book on the French Revolution which Zerajic had torn off and put in his breast pocket. He died while General Varesanin, who was untouched, looked down on him.

I muttered a kind of prayer, that Zerajic hadn't realized in his final minute that his shots had missed.

I looked at the gate lamp, which was a blur, and shook my head and blinked.

I got up and walked through the now quiet streets and lanes of the town. Past the military bakery, shuttered, past the Turkish clock tower and the Begova mosque. Here a soft light shone through the pillared window openings, and there was a murmur of voices. It was Friday evening. Friday, the 12th of June. I began counting off days, and I realized with a shock that the 28th would be a Sunday.

I don't know why it struck me so disastrously, but after that discovery I made straight for Cabri's house. I was lucky, I came upon him at the corner of his street. He took my arm and steered me around. "Let's not run into my father," he said.

"Listen, June 28 is a Sunday."

He stopped under a street lamp and eyed me with surprise.
"Well, yes. So what?"

Bless you and your so-whats, I thought. You're a fourteenth-century schoolbook hero.

40

Minutes of the Prosvjeta Serbian Education Welfare Society,
Sarajevo meeting of Wednesday, June 17, 1914. Prosvjeta minutes. Copied by me. G. P. Gavrilo Princip. Temporary assistant
clerk. Eleven days left. Eleven. E. The treasurer reads his
estimate of the budget. The budget of the Prosvjeta Serbian
etc., etc., Society in Sarajevo for the school year 1914–1915.
1915. Mystical number. Forever to be unknown to me. Budget
for the school year 1914–1915 5,800 crowns. Number of applicants for scholarships 117. Stated needs of those 117 Serbian
education-desiring applicants 34,300 crowns. Average need
per applicant during the school year 1914–1915 293 crowns.
Taking this average as a basis, the treasurer continues. He takes
it as a basis. He draws the conclusion that of the 177 applicants the 19 most worthy. Mr. Bogdanovic asks if no new
funds can be collected this summer. The secretary states that
the 5,800 crowns are an optimistic estimate. Experience has
shown, etc., etc. Our business community is under pressure
from taxation and semi-official charities. It knows that the
authorities do not like our efforts, although officially of course
they are in favor of regional educational activities if only—
The Chairman (interrupting), gentlemen, I suggest we take
our officials at their words spoken officially (Laughter). Secretary (cont'ing), if only such education is loyal to . . . etc.,
etc. Loyal etcetera. The year 1915. The year 1915 dawned on a
freezing morning. On the Bjelasnica Mountain the sun rose
red on the whiteness of the snow, slightly frozen over. A small
animal, hare? deer? runs across the white field. Very long
shadow. Its legs break through the crust once or twice. It will

be. Transfer of mind. Soul? Better to be a hare than not be, not exist. Blood-red coral sun, black unstirring fir tree woods. Only someone from the East can describe the sun and do it justice. Oriente. 117 applicants will divide 5,800 crowns. Each a sausage. A piece of chalk. Debout les damnés de la terre. The Chairman points out. I Gavre Princip and the 116 other applicants. Felix Austria. Maledicta Austria. Maledictum? Is Austria feminine? If the world were mirrored, if Istanbul were in the place of Berlin, the Turks above us, would the Slavs have been like Teutons, would the peasants of the Bavarian mountains curse their Serbian masters? Is that a worthwhile. The secretary announces that the minutes of the budgetary subheading are accepted with the proviso that every effort will be made to augment our funds for the important coming school year 1914–1915. 1915.

It is warm in this room. Flies.

41

My Prosjveta job wasn't full time. I had hours in the library and of wandering through the town. As I was certain that I was to die on the 28th, it seemed strange to me that I still took time to study. But I did, though its strangeness interfered. Every so often, on bad afternoons every five or ten minutes, the thought would make my heart beat like crazy: why put names and ideas in a brain that within a few days will be dead? But I always returned to my work. Most of the books I wanted to read or reread weren't in the town library, of course. Some I owned myself, had taken to Belgrade and carried back again; some I borrowed. A visitor from Belgrade whom we never saw, left a parcel of books at a café of our school days, addressed to "The friends from the Cornerbar." A note said, "Greetings—here are chronicles of great deeds." "Great deeds." They must have come from Djula. One of them was Kropotkin's *History of the French Revolution*, with the boy and his flag on its cover. I tore that off and put it, a bit shakily, in my breast pocket. I, too, would carry that.

As days passed, I didn't get more nervous but calmer. And if I dwell on that, it's not (I hope) as a Young Werther in spite of myself. It's to calm those who'll come after us.

I was almost too calm, for I made Sophia uneasy. She thought I was playing a part and I had to reassure her I wasn't. I was uncomfortable in her presence myself. It tore me in seven different directions. I told myself not to see her often, to avoid suspicion falling on her later. But that wasn't the only reason. Afterward, when all was different from what we had thought, I regretted it mortally not to have hoarded up every possible minute, every image and word connected with her.

Trifko came into town to register with the police as living in Sarajevo—he had no trouble with it—and he and Cabri and I came together, using the library. We felt it was less risky than any secret rendezvous. With the schools closing and exams about over, it was quiet there but not too quiet.

I told my friends now about that messenger supposedly sent from Belgrade. We agreed he might have been a phony, and not much more was said about him. A vicious circle had to be broken, and how could people go on waiting for political awareness if there was nothing to wake them up? This simple idea would play a role in our behavior, afterward. At that time, at our meeting in the dark and dusty library, we did not know there would be an afterward to discuss.

We were sitting at one of the large tables in the corner of the main reading room, near the exit, where there wasn't enough light to read properly and where only old men stationed themselves to doze behind newspapers. The green felt covering of the table was torn; I know the feel of the frayed ends I played with. A warm breath of wind came in through the windows left open at the top. We all had books in front of us by way of props, and we started leafing through these instead of concentrating. We got very distracted at that meeting, even lighthearted. And as for me, I stayed that way after, and I think they did, too.

"In Kosutnjak Park," I felt obliged to bring up, "we agreed

that we would not be formally bound. Perhaps now is the time to ask if any of us has changed his mind."

"Listen to this," Trifko read out. " 'Bender Abbas, a seaport in Persia, owes its name to Shah Abbas who with the English drove the Portuguese in 1622 from Ormiz, destroyed that port, and moved its commerce to Bender Abbas. For a while the new town prospered, but at present it is a wretched place. Population 800.' "

"Come on, Trifko, pay attention to the matter at hand."

"Wouldn't you like to live in a wretched Persian seaport, population 800?"

"I would." I saw the deserted quayside under the vertical, metallic sun, a stretch of beach where it smelled of rotting fish and a dog lay panting in the shade of a broken rowboat, a bar with its beads curtain, pastel liqueurs and unaccountably one bottle of whisky from England, never opened. Out front, a rusty, once white, garden table and chair, never used, too hot to touch. The bar owner a stranded German, no, they wouldn't have an unbeliever in Bender Abbas, he would be a Turk who had seen and tried all the vices of the world and who, somehow, had produced a lovely daughter, never allowed outside, now lying naked on a mat in her upstairs room, no, no daughter, a son, a thin fellow with runny eyes who liked to knock the glowing ashes from his pipe out on the scurfy head of the beggar child. One well, with brackish water, a road full of holes, paved three hundred years ago, running inland into nothingness. Eight hundred people so far from the world that it was unbelievable you could be born there, live and die there, untraceable, untouchable—

"I've been to Ilidza, too," Cabri announced.

"And?"

"And nothing. The Bosna Hotel and the baths are all closed to the public now. My mother liked it. Imagine, she had never been there. She kept saying, 'Look at this, look at that, it's all so solid, there's wealth for you, if only you'd work hard, perhaps one day you'll have your own printing shop. . . .' "

Trifko closed the gazetteer with a thud. "No, of course we haven't changed our minds!" he said. "Let's go drink coffees."

"All together?"

"Sure. To hell with them."

In the town, under a sultry sky, black and yellow Imperial banners were appearing. The sun rays, emerging and vanishing from between black clouds, struck the yellow and made it glitter threateningly.

42

A thunderstorm passed over Sarajevo in the night. When I woke, I could still hear it rumble in the mountains, but Oprankj Street, washed clean, lay in the early sunlight under a dazzling sky. A baker passed by with a basket of bread on his head. Then, an unusual sight in this part of town, a peasant leading a donkey. A street hawker carrying a load of baskets, but without shouting his wares, as if he thought it was too early to wake up people. I looked from my window in both directions along the house wall; it was as if you could feel its warmth from the rows of sleepers sheltered behind it.

That morning I went everywhere, I walked around clutching the town to my heart, everyone in it, and all men. It was summer. The foliage of the trees had become heavy and darkly green, overnight it seemed. Only old, old women were in black that day, everyone else was in bright colors. The Miljacka River was low, and the white pebbles of its bed glistened close to the surface. A great bustle of people, an almost painfully sharp mixture of happiness and restlessness, such as on a warm summer's day fills the streets of towns.

At the police station and the newspaper offices, notices were posted about the visit. The passers-by paid no attention to them, but underneath a police announcement that it was forbidden to throw flowers at the cortege, someone had scribbled, "What a pity." That was outside the office of *Norod*, the only decent Sarajevo paper, never carrying a word about the visit except for a report on the 40,000 crowns spent for that private chapel. The inhabitants of our town were requested to line the route but weren't told yet where that would be. You could easily guess, though, for all along the river quay, men were busy street cleaning, pruning the trees, and hanging banners. At the town hall, the dilapidated fence that had peacefully fallen apart for as long as I could remember was replaced by a new one, painted that same aggressive Austrian yellow.

None of it fazed me. I knew by heart now Zerajic's words on the visit of Francis Joseph, "everybody bowing down . . . a blasphemy against history," and I felt triumphant.

One against a thousand, as in the Andreyev story, and we had already won.

We had already won because we knew that this time Sarajevo was not bowing down.

Only now did I feel happy with our plan, but totally, wildly happy—no exaggeration, this. We had turned the tide. Just think how we would have felt this day if it weren't for our plan, how bitterly powerless. Even if it failed, we would have shown that a man, or a woman, can take destiny in their own hands. We and we alone knew the future; we were as sovereign as an Osmanli who has read in his Book of Life.

Let them hang their banners and print their notices against the throwing of flowers, let them paint over the words written on our walls. Let the town councillors have their morning coats cleaned and brushed, let the shopkeepers put the satrap's portrait amidst their merchandise, and let the mayor start practicing, in front of the mirror, his dishonorable little speech about Bosnia being the newest jewel in the Holy Imperial Crown.

They don't know, they don't know!

43

Unnaturally, the summer weather ended without transition, without thunder. The sky turned white as if a curtain were drawn, and a cold autumn rain began to fall on the town. It came down vertically and with such force that you couldn't keep your eyes open when you looked up against it.

Nor heaven nor earth are at peace. Or some such words. We had read *Julius Caesar* at school. In a frilly German translation, while right in the middle we switched to another play (because the teacher must have stumbled on the chance that Shakespeare's Rome would remind us of our Empire); but I remembered that idea, how when a turnabout is at hand in the affairs of man, nature gets disoriented, too. This unnatural rain. Like a comet, or a sudden flight of vultures. A magical and comforting interrelation.

You could answer that nature wasn't likely to give a damn and that the best thing that could happen to her was if we all killed each other off to the last man. But who was to say? Couldn't some men's lives be in sympathy and harmony with life itself, while others were inimical to it, monsters in the old sense of the word, portents, signs of ill omen?

It was tricky for me to think about the satrap in personal terms. But wasn't he, even as a private man, a destroyer of peoples, an exterminator of animals, as mad as Saint Julian Hospitator, and couldn't that give his death meaning within the logic and harmonies of the earth? Different from Saint Julian, he was not going to redeem himself by ferrying lepers across a wild river. He was no carrier of men; he was a worthy grandson of King Bomba of the Two Sicilies, who bombarded his own town into bloody ruins, from his own citadel, to keep the lowly in line. His father had been that brother of the Emperor, who, I believe, drowned in the river Jordan on his way to Jerusalem, whereto his Society of Jesus confessor had ordered him.

Ominous heirs of mad princes, of those history-book Bourbon and Habsburg ghosts, they were incomprehensibly still alive in Vienna and a perverse current in time was using them to bleed other races. In their medieval center of Europe, from the towns of their Holy Roman Empire, the cobblestoned streets still slippery with the blood of heretics, witches, and Jews, did those German robber barons still rule, and had their nightmare dark castles not yet been turned over to tourists and English-speaking guides.

It was reckless but within the order of nature for students, sons of their most miserable subjects, to face them, to raise their hand against the descendant of a hundred archdukes and archduchesses.

But then again you might say that those princes had Viennese bank accounts and bought and sold their fiefs at a profit, that it was a compliment to call them robber barons, since they were really only American-style capitalists, like those peers who sit with all their titles spread out on the boards of shady British corporations.

I preferred the first version. I knew Cabri would. We did want to raise our hand against the Holy Roman Empire, not against an archducal financier. Maybe the Stock Exchange would replace the House of Habsburg. Not if we could help it. Let us accept that this dismal November rain in June is an omen, foretelling the fall of a mighty house of tyrants. I wanted to leave it that honor. And us.

I marched up a little lane, what they call a sokak in Sarajevo, and stepped with pleasure through the torrents of water that ran down the hill on both sides. Water from the protruding terraces of the houses dripped into my neck. At the top of the lane I came upon a swampy field, beyond it, in a mist of water, sat a row of new infantry barracks. They must have had iron roofs; the rain on it sounded like rifle fire.

As a boy, my secret wish, my only one, had been to be a poet. The poetry I had written, I had never dared show to anyone.

This was the same as being a poet, or more. We were entering on the stage of the world.

44

It was a long and disconcerting journey for the morganatic wife of the satrap, the Duchess Sophie. Morganatic, for though she had been born in Stuttgart as Countess Clotek von Chotkowa und Wognin, the scholasticistic protocol of the court had ruled her to be as unfit to pair her blood with archdukes as if she had been one of those Stuttgart shopkeepers' wives who used to bow so reverently when they waited on her. If it hadn't been for that, she would not have been on this journey: there would have been little reason for her to visit the march provinces of the Empire. Now, these had the attraction that no one would be around who'd take precedence over her. For once, receptions and dinners would be protocolled as they never were in Vienna, without humiliation.

In Vienna, the duchess boarded the Budapest express; from Budapest, she immediately continued south. The train, first following the Danube, veered away, left the Hungarian plains, and started climbing. There was a lengthy, unexplained halt at Stuhlweissenburg, and some hours later a change of trains at Funfkirchen. From there the railroad ran, though in a far from straight line, to Sarajevo. In Sarajevo, another train took her to Ilidza. From Funfkirchen on, it had rained.

It was a tiring journey, especially since she never knew whether the service was simply not better than it was, or whether the railway authorities were putting her in her place. By itself, the vast distances pleased her, for she took a crucial pride in this Empire and its size; she believed implicitly in its system, which had so unhesitatingly rejected her. What disconcerted her in this journey was the startling change in the land, its de-Germanization as she went south. The German names of the railway stops, like the German conversation of her lady attendant, couldn't conceal the reality outside the windows of her compartment. This duchess was not a very perceptive woman. Perhaps it was her traveling by herself to a place she had never been that made her on edge and sensitive. She felt as if the trains were carrying her deeper and deeper into a foreign, inimical country that had no connection with the baroque bedroom in the Belvedere Palace she had left only a day earlier. The trip had looked so cosy on her atlas, all through land colored the same familiar soft pink; the faces, the voices, the mountains outside were so different.

"We're like pioneers, jungle explorers," she had said nervously to her attendant who, not understanding her, had answered, "Indeed, Your Highness."

Once in Ilidza, they realized how hard it was raining. There were porters with umbrellas, but the pavement was muddy and water was spattering and blowing everywhere. A man came up and asked her a question in a foreign language, she did not even recognize which one, and she turned her back on him in her embarrassment and then said sharply to her attendant, "Isn't there German-speaking personnel here?" What a miserable town, she thought, as her carriage rolled through the deserted streets of Ilidza.

The coaches entered a gateway and came to a stop at the garden entrance of the Bosna Hotel. Its director stood on the top step, trying to keep dry. He bowed to her and mournfully looked at the water spots on his new shoes. At his side, a man with a sash across his waistcoat turned out to be not the mayor of the resort but only his adjunct. Rather impudent, she told herself, such a one-horse town could have sent the mayor. I'll complain to Francis about this. No I won't, he has enough to cope with, the poor man.

That last thought brought a gentle smile to her face, which the adjunct mayor assumed was directed at him. She's not half as nasty as they say, he thought.

The director led her up a wide staircase, through a faint smell of cumin-flavored cooking. The apartments prepared for her and her husband were on the second floor, looking down on gardens and a little pond with two swans. He apologized for the bad weather. On clear days, he informed her, the view would reach to the Treskavica and Bjelasnica mountains. She did not answer and turned away from the windows. The Archduke would arrive the following day only, and the hotel director inquired at what hour she wished to dine. "At eight, up here," she told him.

She wandered through the rooms, which had so faultlessly been refurnished in Biedermeier style that you would think you were in Stuttgart or Vienna. She aimlessly picked up the porcelain trinkets, the shepherdesses and silver eggs, and studied the portraits of long-forgotten colonels and generals. At home, it would all have been familiar; in such alien surroundings, this very familiarity discomposed her.

The duchess drank her tea, sitting with her back to the window. It was still only three o'clock. She sent word to serve her dinner at six instead of eight. Three hours to go. She went down into the garden, alone.

A terrible day, terrible, terrible, she muttered. The ground squashed under her feet and the wind tugged at her umbrella. She reached the pond where the swans, unperturbed by the rain, were motionless, staring into an invisible distance; she crossed a row of elms and came to a kind of rotunda.

A curtain of rain and mist hid the panorama, but she thought she could distinguish a dark jagged line over the horizon, the mountains of Bosnia and Montenegro. Birds flying very high overhead, geese, she guessed, cried raw and plaintive cries and fought their way against the wind. Are they already going south?

How strange, the summer has only just begun. She shivered.

45

The satrap, Francis Ferdinand, left Vienna in the early evening. As he was driven to the South Station, the sun had just dipped below the houses. The air was turning cool and under the trees and archways floated the first hint of dusk. Shops and cafés began putting on their electric lights. The streets were crowded.

He felt a vague jealousy for all those people who didn't have to go anywhere, who'd have their coffees or drinks and go home, within the embrace of familiar surroundings.

It was not that he felt apprehensive. He was aware, of course, of the fact that the people of Bosnia and Hercegovina were unwilling subjects of the Empire, but he didn't think there was anything especially different about that from the relation anywhere else between ruler and subject, based on law and discipline rather than disposition. If there was danger, it wasn't something one could reckon with. A rabid fox or squirrel might bite and kill a hunter. Those things were in God's hand.

What had made him nervous and irritable just now with his valet packing his hairbrushes and razors, was another and important matter: the illness of the Emperor Francis Joseph, eighty-four and sick. Rumor had reached him that the court physicians had looked extremely grave that day. He was the successor; any moment now the message would come that summoned him to the Throne. He found it hard to believe that after all those years of waiting, the hour was near. His plans were drafted and he knew who were his enemies, who his friends.

Perhaps, he wondered, it was Providence that he'd be away just now while the Emperor was dying. It would be less muddled that way. He would re-enter Vienna on June the thirtieth, not to visit the sickbed of his Imperial Uncle, but as the new Emperor.

He pulled out a little metal pocket mirror and studied himself thoughtfully. Suddenly he blushed. Without reason, words had entered his mind that he had once overheard, long ago; "The boy is dull-witted," one of his aunts had said about him. "No, just infuriatingly slow," another had answered.

At the station a stream of travelers was emerging onto the square, and again he felt that touch of jealousy for all those people who were almost home.

But Sophie will be waiting for me in Ilidza, he thought.

Night was approaching. Two men were trotting along the sidewalk, lighting the huge ornamental gas lamps. The car drove past the main station entrance and stopped around the corner. His secretary appeared and led him through a side door onto the platform of the Triest express. His itinerary would take him to Ilidza by way of Triest, and included a crossing of the Adriatic by destroyer to the Hercegovina port of Metkovic. He looked forward to that part of the program, more than to the army maneuvers. He had seen to it that his admiral's uniform had been packed for the twenty-four-hour voyage.

The station platform was virtually empty, for it was now half past eight and the train was already three minutes late in leaving: it was him they were waiting for. Some passengers stood at their compartment windows and looked out, but no one seemed to realize who he was. In the well-lit train one car was almost dark, and it was there that his secretary stood still. The satrap frowned; his own private parlor car had no light. A train conductor came running. "A thousand apologies, Your Highness," he said, "we're having trouble with the electricity of Your Highness's car."

"Charming," the Archduke answered and got on.

The corridor was pitch dark, but as his valet opened the door of his sitting room, he saw that half a dozen candles had been lit. They fluttered in the draft and gave an uncertain light.

"They're bringing more candles, Your Highness," he was told by the conductor. "Of course, if Your Highness would prefer a regular first-class compartment . . ." He shrugged and turned away from the man. "It's like a tomb in here," he said to his secretary with a little laugh. He sat down. "Well, that's how we do things in Austria. Good-bye."

The secretary got off and waited on the platform outside for the departure. The train came into motion and he bowed to the Archduke and walked away. It was 8:34.

The train gathered speed and now ran alongside the back gardens of a long row of nondescript houses. There was a level crossing where a man stood swinging a lantern, with one horse-drawn cart waiting, and then another row of houses. The Archduke could look into the kitchens, families sitting around their tables; they still used oil lamps in that quarter of the city. In the dark gardens, lines of laundry hung motionless from tree to tree like signal flags.

As he gestured to his valet to close the curtains, he had his last look at Vienna.

46

I went to the Semiz, the last evening. Jevtic was supposed to be there, but he was not. I drank a bit of wine and didn't talk. At eleven, I walked home. The rains had ended, high clouds were racing across a moonlit sky.

As I undressed, I was yawning. I was pleased with myself because of that.

Everything was done, debts had been paid, and I had written my parents, Sophia, my brother. Bare notes, nothing specific or momentous that could only give trouble with the police for them. I had mailed those after the Saturday collection and they wouldn't go out until Monday.

I lay in bed. I had left my window and curtain open, and stared at the pattern of light on the ceiling.

I didn't have to try to be calm; I was. I tested myself by pursuing unnerving lines of thought. Nothing happened, I came to a halt in the middle. It had all been brooded over so often.

I looked around my room and was happy that I didn't own things. Danilo would take my books, surely, and that's all there was. Something smelly about possessions once their owner is gone. Not the possessions of the peasants, not land or a house that you hold more like a custodian. I mean that pile of things that people collect around them. Trifko had had a prosperous aunt who had a whole house full of stuff no one was allowed to touch. After her death, he described to me, it was embarrassing to sort out those items, all crying "I!" "I!" for an I that had vanished; not-to-be touched and now carried off by the second-hand man. A lower form of human life, self-satisfaction natural only when it's instinct and innocent, like a hermit crab in a shell, eating all it can grab. An innocent bird swallowing worms. I had that from Sophia.

That is not what you should leave behind on earth, things. Exegi monumentum—how did it go? I felt a pang of misery, for that was a favorite quote of mine, that line from Horace about his poems being a stronger monument than—I had forgotten, and that was the end of it, I wouldn't know. There'd be no more chance to look it up.

Never mind. That was an indulgence, too. Nothing could spoil the harmony I felt myself in, with everything, men, women and children, dogs and cats and all other creatures, my brothers and sisters. It may sound like pseudo-Saint Francis of Assisi; I knew perfectly well that my Grahovo Valley silent universe was still there, still silent. But that was just no longer relevant to my life or death.

I put my hands on my body and followed my skin from my chest to my legs. I began stroking my prick, with the precise idea of giving this body, which I had treated as a half enemy, pleasure. It didn't rise. There wasn't any tension, only a friendly warmth of contact.

The bells of the Catholic cathedral struck midnight. It was Sunday. They were unusually loud; perhaps because the wind was from that direction. Then I waited for the Serbian Orthodox Church, always a minute later, a darker, rumbling sound. A long silence, and the hoarse clock tower of the Begova mosque —not striking twelve, though, but three. Three o'clock in the mysterious Turkish time brought to Sarajevo from the East. All those different God seekers in one Serbian town, wanting to be heard. Only the Jews of Sarajevo kept silent. Why had the synagogue no chimes to strike the hour of Jerusalem? I would never know.

The people, as distinct from priests, pastors, and mullahs, were also voiceless in the night.

I dreamed. I heard someone say quite clearly, "The dream of irreversibility." Perhaps it was me who said it. Those words seemed so profound that I tried to wake myself, to write them down. But I couldn't wake up. I saw a series of images in which things precisely were reversed: a burning house, the fire went out and the house was whole again; a dead woman who got off a bier, blew out the candles around it, and was alive; pieces of stone that flew upward and came together as a pot on a shelf, a pot I had broken as a child in Grahovo. But that voice, my voice, repeated, "the irreversibility of a deed."

Then I heard the bells of Sarajevo ring again, and I dreamed that I was the tongue of a bell, that I hung inside it and kicked the metal with great force. It wasn't a real dream, for I wanted to dream that, I had thought it up. When I wanted to stop it, I couldn't, though. I hung by my feet then, and my head was striking the bronze, without pain but with a great deafening resonance obliterating my mind.

47

I softly closed the front door behind me and stood in Oprkanj Street. It was not yet eight o'clock, Sunday morning, and very still. You could feel it was going to be a hot day.

As I let go of that door, a tremor ran through me. Here I was, on the street, on the day, ready. Then I caught my breath.

No one was about, but I made myself move nonchalantly anyway, like a man strolling with no place in particular to go. In the middle of the empty street, I did my check several times in a row. Right hand in my right pocket, to feel the Browning, push the safety catch off and back on, and tell from the smooth viewing groove that there is a cartridge in the chamber. Same hand under my jacket on the left, touch the cap of the grenade tucked in my belt. Left hand in my left jacket pocket, to hold a little medicine bottle with the cork half out: HCN. Browning, grenade, poison. Browning, grenade, poison.

It would sound desperate if you read it in a newspaper account. Yet it was simple. We had managed. I was one step higher on the wide marble staircase I had first imagined in Belgrade, one step only from the top.

I met Trifko and Cabri at the cake shop on Cumurija Street. We knew where each of us would post himself. Everything had been said. But we wanted a last look at one another.

I sat down at their table and made a face at the large pastry with whipped cream Trifko was eating. "It's his third," Cabri said. We laughed. Erma the waitress said to me, "You're so neat, too. Are you all going to a wedding?"

A young boy came over and Cabri said this was his good friend Tomo. "I'm just off," he told him.

"Where to?"

"I'm going to have my picture taken."

"Really? On a Sunday?"

"Do you think I don't plan things in advance?" Cabri asked him. "Joseph Schrei is open on Sundays."

"Can I come, too?" the boy asked.

Cabri stood up. "Yes, sure," he said. "We'll have one taken together."

I got up after him and waited in the doorway till he had paid. "Are you serious," I said.

Cabri smiled. He held the door open and I followed him out. He bent his head close to mine and added, but in a light, calm voice, "I want something of me to remain."

I watched him walk down the street with Tomo and slowly followed. At the corner I realized I hadn't said good-bye to Trifko. Oh, well, perhaps better.

The only part of the route that was definite was Appel Quay along the river.

The satrap, arriving by special train from Ilidza at 9:45, would first inspect the new garrison barracks near the station and then be driven to the town hall for his municipal welcome. The town hall is adjacent to the Miljacka River, and the cortege would travel the full length of the quay. After that, he would go back along Appel Quay, and probably through Francis Joseph Street, to open the new state museum on Cemalusa. From there, he'd go for the lunch and reception by the governor of Bosnia, General Oskar Potiorek, his personal appointee, a notedly dumb general and very efficient pursuer of Germanification. Potiorek had his residence in a large park south of the river between the Latin and Emperor Bridges. Unless they were to wind through a maze of back streets, the cortege would again have to follow the quay.

After I had left the cake shop, I took a detour, avoiding Francis Joseph Street, which leads to that new museum. I walked all around and got to Appel Quay across from the College Bridge, on the corner of the Bank for Austria-Hungary. I stepped into its vestibule and stood in the archway of white and brown marble, under a bas-relief in black of the Emperor. It was ice cold in there, after the warm sun.

Appel Quay lay in front of me, still virtually deserted in both directions. Perhaps it was all those black and yellow banners, perhaps it was the way I saw it that morning, but the quay was different, not hostile, but alien, unknown. It brought to my mind the lake avenue of Lucerne, of which I had seen a large photograph in the railway station. It doesn't look in the least like Lucerne, I thought; what is there to make me think of it so insistently.

A few people were standing here and there in the shadow of the little trees and buildings as if already waiting to see the cortege drive by. They were all men, though, all in Sunday suits, and I decided they were detectives. I wondered if it were conspicuous to hang around in that bank vestibule until there would be more passers-by and spectators. Walking away, up the street again, might look even stranger.

Then I saw a young man whom I recognized come across the College Bridge. I had been in third grade with him, and he used to look as dapper at that time as he did now. His name was Maxim and he was the son of Judge Francis Svara, Chief Prosecutor of the Tribunal of Sarajevo. He turned right onto the quay, and I had fallen in step with him before he had even seen me. I greeted him with enthusiasm and he frowned, surprised, for he had been the kind of boy we avoided. His good manners, or the nice sunshine, triumphed, and he smiled back and said, "Don't tell me you got here this early to welcome the Heir to the Throne."

"Did you?"

"Oh, I—my father will take me to the Governor's reception later. It's an official function, of course," he added, with what sounded like a note of apology in his voice. "I'm on my way to the nine o'clock mass."

I couldn't think of anything to say but "I see." I walked on close beside him, as if we were bosom pals, and I saw one of those men in the shadow begin to tip his hat to Maxim and then think better of it and stare over our heads. Maxim was an ideal escort.

"I'm going to the University of Zagreb this fall," he told me. "And maybe, maybe even to Budapest."

I wanted to give a chatty answer, but to my frustration I

just couldn't get one out. I opened my mouth, closed it, and gave him another smile.

We had now passed two or three of those little clusters of detectives. "What are your plans?" Maxim asked. He was really being friendly.

I shrugged and smiled once more.

When we reached the Latin Bridge, Maxim, who must have thought I wasn't quite right in the head, said, "Well, I turn here, good-bye, Gavrilo," and hastened away.

I stood alone on the sidewalk, facing Schiller's Delicatessen. I went in, and with my hands in my pockets started to study the labels of his wines.

48

I'd always been intrigued by those triangular chocolate tablets Schiller had in his window, from Switzerland, with a picture of mountain flowers on the wrapping—that equilateral shape seemed a special refinement. Now, after having looked at everything there for as long as I could, I finally bought one, and discovered it was like a comb, triangles of chocolate a finger apart from each other. It was half air. That's expensive chocolate.

It was busier now on Appel Quay. Few people stood along the embankment in the sun, which was already high, but along the houses was a line of onlookers, real ones, not just detectives. And then there were the normal passers-by. I felt protected by their numbers, and by the half-unwrapped chocolate bar in my hand. It looked good. I heard a policeman ask a woman walking past with a bouquet what it was for. She stared at him. The police department must have been obsessed by that flower-throwing edict. They tend to latch on like that to one specific. To our advantage.

And no troops so far. At the visit of Francis Joseph, his entire route had been lined with them. Rather a slight to Francis Ferdinand, unless he was supposed to be that much more popular and safe. But he had just attended two days of army maneuvers. Perhaps his guards were coming into the town with him. Even if they were, that would not be as effective security as if they were placed beforehand.

I watched those Sunday strollers on their way to outings or churches or come to see the live face of our future ruler, so terribly well known to us from a never-ending series of pictures, the head with its right angles, the back of it straight down, the heavy upturned mustaches, oddly without any likeness to the man who was his Imperial Uncle several times over.

I felt a stranger among them, a traveler. No, not a traveler, a pilgrim.

I discovered a notion of contempt within me, contempt for these men and women pursuing their daily dailinesses. Their unawareness of the moment.

I caught snatches of conversation, nasty rain, nice weather, pork roast for dinner, children home with colds. You could tell from the way they were dressed who had made his peace with the Empire, and they were many; they were commemorating Vidovdan in Vienna-fashion bell suits with English stripes, pointed shoes and Panama hats with rainbow ribbons. I was in a world of my own in which none of these people had a part. Like the contempt a painter feels for those who cannot see beauty. Or a lover for a husband.

But I was not in a world of my own. Cabri was standing somewhere farther west along that quay. Trifko. And there were others.

Not a feeling of contempt.

Their eyes would be opened.

I asked a man what time it was.

"Just after ten," he said, and at that moment the cannon of the fortresses on the hills encircling Sarajevo started firing. A twenty-four-gun salute echoing back and forth over the town mastered by those guns.

49

The satrap was on his way.

One of those black-suited detectives stepped forward from his tree shadow, took off his hat and shouted, "Hurrah." His neighbors looked at him in surprise. I moved to the edge of the sidewalk and looked down the quay.

Drifts of military music from somewhere in the silence that followed the cannon. A vast flock of crows, raised by that salute, circling and circling over the river, a circular black rush, dizzying against the blueness of the sky.

Then I heard the explosion, far off, shouting, and people began to run west toward the College Bridge. I crossed over, and an automobile full of police officers went by behind me, almost hitting me, unaccountably driving east, away from the sound. I ran along the embankment toward it. I could see a car in the distance with a large Imperial banner on the left of its hood, and it had come to a stop.

It had been Cabri's grenade, and it had succeeded. I knew.

Policemen who had been standing along the sidewalk poured across the road and stopped us. All I could see were the backs of people, pushing. Then the circle opened, and I saw Cabri. His face was bloody and he was dragged along by four or five men, in uniform and in black detective Sunday suits. He was at least fifty feet down the quay from me.

I worked my way toward him, with my right hand in my pocket and the safety catch off.

My task now was to shoot him, and then myself.

When I had come to within fifteen feet, I caught Cabri's eyes. He could not see my hand, still in my pocket, but he understood the expression on my face.

I was going to do what he would have done in my place.

He looked steadily at me and slowly shook his head.

His grenade had failed.

A sound of car engines starting up. We were hastily pushed toward the houses, and then the cortege drove by at great speed. I counted four or five cars, all but one of them open. I did not see the satrap.

The police with Cabri followed, moving at the double.

Everyone around me was talking at the same time, but there was no undue excitement. I saw a man beside me whom I knew, an actor I think. "That was an idiotic thing to try," he said to me.

"Yes."

I was back at Schiller's. Two children stood staring in his windows. I gave them the chocolate tablet.

50

My most precise thought of that moment was that I had to pee. I went around to the back street in the rear of the shop. No one. I stepped behind a tree. I spit right through the arc; as a child I used to think that meant good luck.

Chaos. Cabri in their hands. Trifko nowhere to be seen. Would they cancel the ceremonies? Wouldn't they be afraid to cave in like that? Yes, they would. They couldn't sneak the satrap out of Sarajevo like a thief. If they did, it would be the beginning of an unraveling of the Empire. They couldn't I had to count on that. Our plan was now only, now precisely, the only possible outcome of events. We moved within the logic of time. The marble staircase.

I reappeared at the corner. Appel Quay was almost empty and it looked hot and dusty.

It looked pathetic. A Serbian village street, force-fed into being a capital avenue of the Austrian Empire. A mistake that would doom them.

In front of Schiller, which has its door on Francis Joseph Street, a small crowd was still gathered and the policemen walking along the embankment didn't even look at them. A lady was sitting in a chair brought out from the shop, fanning herself.

Church bells chimed half past ten, the hour set for the museum opening. I tried to think by what other route they could go there; I tried to visualize where I might stand or hide near the Governor's house later. Suddenly Trifko stood at my side. A wave of warmth swept through me. "Thank heaven," I whispered, "don't worry, we'll do it. It is Vidovdan." He stared at me with blank eyes.

It wasn't Trifko at all, it was a boy who didn't the least look like him. I muttered, "I'm sorry," and moved away.

Then reality began to leave me. I was half sick, half dizzy. A reaction to seeing Cabri, bloody and alive, in the power of the police. No, it wasn't.

It was an anticipation, an icy awareness of time slowing down. I didn't know what it meant. I tried to swallow and couldn't.

An automobile came toward us from the east, from the town hall. It braked, turned and drove right past us, up Francis Joseph Street! It was the one that had almost hit me, with the police officers. Another car followed, open, with army officers, ignoring us, talking to each other.

Dust blew down the street. The crows, circling, would never again come to rest. I saw a policeman stiffen and salute. A third car approached.

It was going fast, but not in a straight line; I thought it was zigzagging although I knew that couldn't be. It drove close to the embankment. A man and a child standing there lifted their arms and waved. I saw its two big, round, lamps look toward me. The sun sparkled on the brass rings around their glass. The car was open; I saw the face of the chauffeur, under a dark cap, behind the upright large windshield. That, too, was fitted in a brass frame, throwing off sparks of light.

Like the others before, this car slowed down and turned toward us. The black and yellow Imperial standard fluttered over the dark green hood. I recognized General Potiorek on the folding seat, and in the back, dazzling white against the white hood and the bright air over the river, a hat, of the duchess, and a blur of green feathers, the medieval helmet of the satrap.

Insanely, I lost time staring at the standard, noticing for the first time in my life that it had a border of red and black triangles, and the two-headed eagle that looks, looks—I had the Browning out, pointed, the car had gone by, and tears of anger and grief were rolling down my face.

In that instant, the car stopped.

This was so mysterious it had to be imaginary. It is what I wanted to will, to will the stopping and reversing of time. To get back to that lost split second in which I alone could have saved—

The car began backing up, past me. An Imperial battue, for me.

A glass dome fell over that car and me, excluding all else. The air turned into crystal. No one could move.

I saw the running board with its tool box in a leather strap, the driver looking back, away from me, over his left shoulder. On the far running board, an Austrian army officer, looking back, too. General Potiorek, in a two-dimensional profile. In the right-hand back seat, the woman, in a white dress under a white hat with feathers, staring straight ahead. Beside her, a space of buttoned leather, black and gleaming with sunlight reflected from the vertical windshield, transfixing me. But though motionless, I forced my eyes from that ribbon of leather to the man in the left corner.

He was in a blue uniform. He sat up straight and he looked fat, his uniform was a wrinkled cylinder shape without waist. The sun shone through the green plumes of his helmet.

He was a stranger, untouchable. Our discussions had nothing to do with this man. It would be impossible to attain him; we had fooled ourselves.

Then I heard shouts and screams.

And the satrap turned his head toward me, and I looked into his eyes, pale blue and bulging eyes. Not fish eyes, a man's eyes.

I turned my head away; I had to. I pulled the trigger twice before a saber struck the pistol out of my hand. Another blow got me on the shoulder, and my grenade fell out of my belt on the sidewalk, followed by me.

I sat on the sidewalk and I had my cyanide bottle in my hand. Military boots were around me but a Serbian voice cried at them in German, "Why don't you get out of here!" I looked up and saw against the sky a saber lifted above me, and the hand and arm of a man who warded it off, for me. My blessed people, I love you. I had the cork out with my teeth and swallowed the liquid. I awaited darkness and I was happy.

But it did not come. I was not dead.

51

I was not dead. Men were striking me and pulling me up and I could not pass out. My mouth burned as if I had drunk lye. Cabri, the same must have happened to him. What had they given us? The Vidovdan sacrifice, our passion play, destroyed by a pharmacist. I cried.

I was dragged along Appel Quay. Shouts, running feet, car engines. Uniforms all around me, German-speaking voices only. I blinked and saw a man standing a few feet ahead, with a raised walking stick. I couldn't duck and he beat me with it. I couldn't see any more from blood dripping into my eyes. But I felt very little.

We were going up steps. A flash of yellow on the side. It was the town hall. A door, a bench, and then I could see again. An orderly was wiping my face with a towel he dipped in a bowl of liquid. Alcohol or carbolic acid. Great pain.

They pulled me up again and through another door, and I was held upright in front of an empty desk.

Someone came in, a movement of black from the door to the desk. I managed to wipe my face against my sleeve while they held my arms, to get the acid or alcohol out of my eyes.

The black shape said he was the Investigating Judge of the Sarajevo District Court. He asked my name, age, and nationality.

I couldn't answer. My mouth was too swollen, tears ran down my face, and I'd have fallen if they had not held me.

"I charge you now with premeditated assault on the Heir Apparent," my judge said. "State your name, age, nationality, and motives."

The men shook me. "Answer the judge."

I closed my eyes.

Bells began to ring into that room. The dark sound of church bells entered the room, reverberated from wall to wall, turned the air into a whirlpool that held me upright without support.

I opened my eyes. It was a pale, puffy man behind the desk. A narrow, long room with two windows; the shutters had been closed and someone had pushed them only half open; a mantelpiece with a clock, half past eleven; a mahogany desk, an inkwell; a calendar on the wall, the Emperor, a Chinese print. All in vibration, glowing with the tremor of those bells, all the bells of Sarajevo.

A man came in and walking with difficulty against that sea of sound rolling in through the windows, approached the judge and whispered in his ear. The judge stood up, looked at a paper, and then at me.

"Lock him in," he said, "and stay with him. Put him in chains."

We stood and waited. A pain of waiting.

"You—" he said, in German suddenly, "you have killed the Archduke Francis Ferdinand."

I sat on a stool, with chains on my wrists and ankles. I sat up straight. Two policemen sat on a bench, our knees almost touching. They stared at me a while, and then they looked out of the little barred window. It was silent.

"Here comes Pfeffer," one said to the other.

Judge Pfeffer came in. I stood up. He asked his questions again and I told him who I was. He took a paper out of the inside pocket of his coat, and read, "I open against you the investigation of the crime of murder, committed by you today, in that you shot treacherously and from the closest distance, with a Browning pistol, at the Heir Apparent and his wife, the Duchess of Hohenberg, with the intention to kill them, and that you hit them both, causing their deaths a short time afterward; I now commit you to preliminary imprisonment according to the paragraphs 184 and 189 of the penal code of the Empire."

He turned around. I said, "We had no intention of killing the Duchess of Hohenberg. I did not shoot at her. I regret her death."

He had gone. The policemen left, too, and barred the door.

52

The silence deepened still more.

I thought about his words. The crime of murder. Treacherously. They shriveled away. They were lies, although they were Judge Pfeffer's truths. Nothing could make him believe that their truths were our lies.

Where you are born. A baby snatched from a Bosnia mountain farm and taken to Belvedere Palace, will grow up a Habsburg. It is they who need more than their share, it is they who have put the world in a state of siege.

There was no terror linked with us. We had thrown ourselves in its path.

The death of his wife; I waited to feel horror. I did not. She had not come to Sarajevo as a wife but in another role.

The door opened with much clanking, and one of the policemen came back in. I wondered what would happen. He motioned me to stand up, took away my stool, and left again. I sat on the floor in an intense sensation of tranquillity.

My body didn't bother me. I had never felt so clearheaded. I was addressing a tribunal.

Don't ask us now for shame or pity.

We have shown the meaning human life has for us by offering ourselves in exchange.

That way, as always, we were more generous than you. We could have planned our escapes.

For the man who was chauffeured down that dusty quay,

waved at by a passer-by in a straw hat and a child in a sailor's suit, had no business being a sad human being in a wrinkled uniform. He had no business being a family man. Ruling from a thousand miles' distance, putting millions in his jeopardy, he should have been a god. His subjects had every right to test his immortality.

If Francis Ferdinand of Austria-Este and the Duchess of Hohenberg were not immortals, were subject to death and subjects of pity, then their roles and deeds had been a monstrous masquerade.

I got to my feet, which was difficult now, and looked up through the window. I saw a bit of sky not bigger than a hand, but the blue of our sky on a late Sunday afternoon, when the light seems to gather from everywhere, and when it lasts on and on.

It had really happened. I wasn't theorizing. Our abstract plan had turned into two deaths, into telegrams flying along the lines of Europe, into us two in our cells. You can't realize such a thing beforehand. It's only words then, like a priest depicting heaven and hell.

How to put your hands on it, how to give it substance. In the hills, the Vidovdan dancing would have begun, carbide lamps would have been lit in the tents where they sell brandy and roast meat. And then gendarmes in black uniforms would appear and call the musicians aside. The dancers would stand still and stare as the musicians picked up their instruments and left without a word.

For telegrams would have reached every police post, east to the Bukovina, south to Novi Bazar, and messengers would go out at once. The protocol of the Empire could not tolerate music on this day anywhere within its borders.

A hush, a listening.

The streets of Sarajevo in this sunset, just outside my window.

I couldn't believe that no matter how hard I'd want to, I'd never again find myself on them. Never again to set foot on them. It was harder to grasp than being dead would have been.

53

I had forgotten to put the Kropotkin book cover in my pocket, that Sunday morning, the morning of this same day, another age. I realized it when it was almost dark and I decided to have a last look at it before they'd take it away from me. I was mad at myself, but my mistake served me. Through the night, as they repeated two or three questions and beat me up, I kept thinking of the boy with the red flag and the waving hair in that picture. He has his mouth half open, not as if he were shouting, though, and he looks sad rather than either angry or enthusiastic. But his sadness has a strength that completely convinces you, and you know it is as it should be and that other feelings would be gratuitous.

I tried to nurse that same strong sadness in myself. It didn't work totally but quite a lot. To my own surprise, I wasn't too much affected by the police harassing me. I concentrated on the boy on the book cover and on all that lay behind that. I saw him more and more clearly. I recognized him now from a painting of the Paris Commune that is reproduced in a Belgrade library book.

Why sadness? I don't know exactly. There were moments of bitter aloneness, and other moments when the room was the center of Bosnia, friends, everyone, watching me and counting on me. That's when I couldn't help smiling, and the sergeant opened a drawer and brought out what looked like pumice stone. It was silver caustic, the stuff kids use to burn off warts. He pulled the plasters away, which the orderly had stuck on my head, and rubbed the injuries with it.

I am not martyrizing myself. They did much worse to Trifko, as I learned later, and anyway I am thinking back to this through a thick screen of detachment. You don't remember how pain feels. I do remember that things got confused after the caustic and I wasn't coherent any more.

Later that night they put me in a closed cart, with a soldier holding a rifle, and we drove to an infantry barracks in the hills. There they took away my tie, shoelaces and so forth, put me in heavier chains than before, and locked me in a cell of their military prison. I was too thirsty to sleep, but I lay on the cot in the darkness and peace returned to me. I had reached the top of my marble staircase. It was us who had decided, long ago in Kalemegdan Park, that we would die. Wisely we had made ourselves invulnerable. They could do nothing.

54

That cell had a window at eye level. It looked out on a large, walled courtyard. I stood there from the first light but nothing stirred.

I heard an irregular tapping on the wall to the left of me, stopping and starting, but I didn't pay attention to it.

Steps now came down the corridor and doors opened and closed. The peephole in my door showed an eye, and then the hatch was shoved back and the head of a man was visible behind it. He wasn't a guard but a trustee or something, for under a soldier's cap he had an unshaven face, and a grin on that face. He handed me a tin cup and a slice of bread, and before closing the hatch he pointed with his left thumb to my wall and grinned even wider.

I sat on the cot and put my ear against that wall. The tapping had stopped. Had he meant that Cabri was in the cell beside me? Was it the Stepnyak code? We all knew from Stepnyak's book how you put the alphabet in a square of five by five letters, leaving out the *q*, and then you gave the vertical place of a letter with short, sharp, knocks and the horizontal place with heavy ones. Thus one sharp and one heavy knock spells A.

I hastily drank the liquid in the cup. I had to see the letters in front of me to work this. I drew them on the wall as well as I could, with my finger and the dirt from the floor. Then I used my cup to tap out "Cabri."

The answer came, "Gavre."

We were next to each other and we could talk.

Tin cups, judas holes in doors, shackles, tapping on walls—what we had read about all those years, of the Russian revolutionaries, the prisoners of the Czar. Read with jealousy because they were so clear about their goals and so loving to each other. Now it was real for Cabri and me. We surely hadn't foreseen that when we discussed Stepnyak. I remember Cabri saying he'd go crazy, waiting a minute for each word.

Here we ourselves were part of a continuity, at the end of a chain of hundreds or thousands, starting back with Babeuf and Saint-Just or as much further back as you wanted.

I asked Cabri if they had hurt him badly.

He tapped, "Im alright. You."

"Me too."

"Others."

"Dont know."

Then he tapped, "Hurrah for us."

55

That innocence ended an hour later. Shouts and curses sounded from the courtyard. I saw men brought in there, businessmen, shopkeepers, students, clerks, Serbs all, from the look of them. They were pushed by soldiers who on the command of an invisible officer or NCO trotted along the wall and came to a stop when they had surrounded the Serbs. Then they turned and faced them.

They were the soldiers from the marches of the Empire, the mercenaries and reservists who have been turned against any other man until they can see him suffer and die unmoved, with blank eyes, with no feeling but the dumb caution that is created within a violent bureaucracy. There they stood, with their thin mustaches like two leeches painted on the upper lip, the field-gray kepis with black visors, gray tunics with breast pockets in a double curve like the tent roof of Tartars, the cartridge pouches sitting on the middle of their stomachs, and the rifles with short bayonets fixed, pointed at those people herded in their circle.

More and more prisoners were brought in until they must have numbered as many as two hundred. Some of them tried to sit down on the ground and were promptly prodded back onto their feet with rifle butts.

By and by it got very still. The sun had topped the barracks and fell into the yard. The Serbs and the soldiers looked at one another.

The sun climbed; you could see the air starting to vibrate with heat in the corners made by the wall.

I turned away and sat on my cot. One second later, a guard opened the door, told me to get off, and hooked the cot up against the wall. "Do that first thing in the morning," he said. "You're not here for a rest cure."

Back to the window. A swaying and murmuring as if these men were a human wheat field in the wind.

I tapped, "Reprisals."

Cabri answered, "Fucking Schwaben."

Commands outside. New soldiers appeared and took over from the first batch. The same bayonets, mustaches, and eyes.

A gate in the wall of the yard opened. An officer started to shout. I couldn't hear the words, for beyond the bars of my window was a pane of glass. He vanished again.

I walked slowly up and down, dragging the chain.

An endless summer day, impossible to believe it would ever be evening.

Men outside fainted in the heat. One or two were carried away. Others were left where they lay. A man near me pissed in his pants. He didn't dare move, a puddle formed at his feet. His face turned red.

The trustee with the grin appeared and brought me another slice of bread and a cup with a kind of coffee. He pointed at my window and, still grinning, shook his head. That meant out there they wouldn't get anything. He wasn't sadistic, I'm sure; he thought I'd appreciate my meal more that way.

I stood and stared at those men.

A bugle sounded. I unhooked my cot and lay down again. I was crouched, ready to jump up at the sound of the door. But it finally got dark and no one had come.

At dawn, I shuffled to the window. The Serbs were gone. The courtyard was empty but for a black felt hat and a shoe, and puddles of vomit or shit.

But as I stood there, the same shouts were heard and the same soldiers trotted back into their circle position. This time it was peasants who were herded in, maybe two dozen in all. These all sat down on the ground and no one interfered. One of them picked up the felt hat and shoved it in his blouse.

I held on to the stone edge of the window sill. My father. My brother. Other soldiers entered the yard and they carried spades, wooden beams, and tools. They started to dig holes, and the beams were hammered together into L shapes with a short oblique beam to strengthen the L. They made three of those, and then they lowered each one into a hole, and watered and stamped the ground tightly around them.

They had erected three gallows.

I saw the peasant who had picked up the hat pull it out again and let it fall to the ground.

They brought a table and kitchen chairs. An officer appeared smoking a cigarette, but looking at his prisoners, he dropped it and stepped on it. A bad sign. Officers don't show such respect for live peasants.

The sun was high now.

One of the peasants was made to stand up and come toward that table. I didn't think a word was spoken. The soldiers all seemed to keep their lips tight together. The peasants seemed to mumble to themselves or just stand with open mouths. They bound the peasant's hands behind his back. He frowned and blinked at the sun as if that was all that was bothering him.

A sergeant with his rifle flung over his shoulder came into my view. He held a piece of string and a towel, and he tied the string to its corners, working with slow, clumsy movements. Then he bound that string around the peasant's forehead. He turned it and the peasant's face vanished behind the towel. I thought his last look was in my direction. I may have shouted. Or Cabri. One of the soldiers lifted his rifle and suddenly fired a shot. I heard the bullet hit the wall.

I ducked. Silence.

When I looked again, from the corner of that window, nothing had changed, no one looked our way. Perhaps there had been no shot.

The peasant was standing motionless under the center gallows. The towel hung over his face and covered him from his hair almost to his middle. It hung straight down, it made him appear to be already no longer a man, but an anonymous something, a puppet, or an Arab in a children's masquerade.

Then that man, that blinded entity, started crossing himself. A doll, pointing blindly at the four edges of a towel.

The Catholic Empire cursing itself.

Two soldiers put a rope around his neck, passing it under the towel from hand to hand.

Two others made him climb a chair.

56

I was taken to Judge Pfeffer. He said he had opened the investigation. He said that Trifko and Danilo had been arrested. We better speak up now for our own good.

I said the police were beating me.

He told me, no. Impossible. Under the benefit of the Austrian law—

I took a step forward, bent my head toward him and pointed at the gashes on my forehead. I could feel them ooze. "Here's the proof," I said.

Judge Pfeffer had turned blind and deaf. The gendarme pulled me back.

I wondered what the others would do. We had not planned for this. There was to be no afterward. And I had not been thinking about it, nor even about the satrap, or anything like that. I thought about the peasant with the towel hanging straight down in front of his face and the wooden movements with which he commended his mortal soul to no one.

That jerky sign of the cross had wiped our theories out of my mind.

Who was I to be looking at the Investigating Judge of the District Court of Sarajevo when I should see nothing but gray daylight filtering through a dirty towel. Why was I standing in a carpeted room, facing a desk, a calendar, a portrait of the Emperor, instead of on the hot cobblestones of a courtyard. Why was a clerk writing down my words instead of them choking in my mouth. I had tried to stick my hand in the iron wheel grinding away. And still, in that inexorable system, I was better than those men in the courtyard. It was better to lift your hand against the Brahmins than to be an untouchable.

It must be that they were the personifications of violence. Thus they respected even counterviolence more than humility. Who does not take up the sword shall perish by the sword. If Judge Pfeffer looked at me with contempt, it was not because I had killed the satrap but because of our motives. He could be judge to another satrap, but not to our brotherhood.

Wouldn't it be vainness for us to accept their evaluation, to accept our roles in this rite? Perhaps I was even now not so different from the students in the Semiz, drinking wine and discussing girls instead of assassination. Suppose our dedication had just been monstrous vanity? I felt my blood draw away from my head. What right did I have to be less nameless than that peasant who was hanged from a kitchen chair under my cell window? He was already buried. His name would be in no newspaper; his existence on earth was already near forgotten.

The gendarme shook me. Judge Pfeffer had been waiting for an answer to a question. Now he looked at me and asked, "Are you sick?"

I did not want to partake of the benefits of Austrian law.

Our assassination had not been a recognizing of them, had not been an inverse obeisance.

"We do not know you," I said. "You are anonymous enemies and we are anonymous peasants. All you will need for us are towels and kitchen chairs."

57

The wall. Between Cabri and me was a one-foot thickness of stone, irregular blocks cemented together. There were porous spots on which a kind of lichen grew, but under those and everywhere else the stone was as hard as iron. It always felt moist, even during the short spell in the afternoon when the sun shone right through my window and made the cell hot as an oven. This thick, ironlike, sweating wall became the link between Cabri and me. We shook hands through that wall; we talked through it. There are no human absolutes. The short and heavy taps on the stone became speech, and a word a minute became the speed of speech. What a fitting tempo in a cell where a morning hour lasted a day and a day had no evening. How different language became when each letter took its own time and place, when you wondered if "we" would remain "we" or become "week" or "were." It was talking like a blind man walking, aware of each step, change and form, but in an agony to grasp the whole. We were close to each other. Our wall was a river on which we set words adrift, letter by letter, and waited for the other to pick them up. We had pledged ourselves not to survive. July 1: we were not meant to see the sun rise on that day, neither of us. That is why we could talk so well; we lived together in one supernaturally elongated second between swallowing the cyanide from our little bottles and death.

"Acid did not work," Cabri had tapped. He was beautifully precise and regular; you could tell he was a typesetter. He had simply substituted sound for metal; language for him must already have been, letters first.

"No."

"So let us instead," Cabri went on, "speak suicidal."

I was not sure what he meant, and I answered, "But I want to be anonymous like—" I intended to go on, "anonymous like the peasants with their heads behind those towels," but I got confused with my code and stopped. Cabri was continuing:

"We arent Russian revolutionaries. Bosnia is very small and no one will know of us or understand. We must explain. Propaganda by the deed. We must tell everything."

I did not answer immediately. Cabri tapped, "Wait," and a long silence followed. He came back and tapped, "Trifko is on the other side of me. Danilo next to him."

Four of us, side by side, linked by walls. Could they have done this on purpose, would they have some old trustee listen in to those knocks on the stone? The code was simple enough. But what could they gain? I had no more secret.

I signaled, "All must consider."

Cabri: "What."

What? A vague and complicated dilemma, too damn complicated perhaps. This is what I'd have to put in letters and taps on the wall: "We can atone for the victims of the Austrian reprisals who die unknown only by remaining nameless too, by remaining mute. By being peasants and not brave clever private persons. On the other hand—" Oh hell, I thought. On the other hand, indeed. Fourteen letters right there, seventy taps. Who needs it. The wall wants pureness and simplicity.

Now even the dilemma smelled of indulging in private dramatics. Vanity, once removed. You don't become nameless by choice; my father wouldn't know what was the matter with me. Like abandoning an outpost in a battle.

I: "Agree. We must explain ourselves. Some of it will get out into the open."

There was no answer. I didn't know if Cabri was waiting for me to go on or if he was speaking with Trifko at the other wall. I redrew my alphabet which was fading, and waited. From far away, from the infantry barracks, there was a stirring of voices. I thought I could distinguish the sound of horses and carts. It wasn't that far, actually, but there were many walls. We had so often looked up at these barracks looming over us. Then, too, silent prisoners must have been hidden in them.

Cabri gave one loud bang on the wall.

I signaled, "But then I do not know how to cope with the reprisal dead. Our guilt. They were not asked."

Cabri: "If we speak fully we will protect the innocent. The others feel the same."

I only answered, "No." I didn't believe it. The Austrians weren't trying to punish a crime; it was their secret war waged on Bosnia that we had forced into the open. If the poison had worked, there'd still have been those hangings.

Or would there? I was dizzy. I did not know any more.

I sat on the floor with my eyes closed. Cabri had started speaking, but I had missed the beginning and couldn't follow him. He went on for very long and when he had stopped, I tapped out, "Repeat." I smiled, I could imagine his indignant expression at that. He answered in telegram style:

"No guilt. War of people. Only sin is sacrificing others while not self."

I was exhausted. I tapped, "Yes."

"What will you tell the judge?" Cabri asked.

"That I am a Serbian hero."

We no longer got bread and coffee at night, but mess tins with soup. That evening I found a message scratched at the bottom of my tin. It was signed Trifko and read, "Friends, forgive me for not firing. No chance. For trying to escape after. Arrested at border." I thought about that. I wrote under it, "Yes! To Danilo: my terrible mistake, I gave my address. G."

The moment I had handed my tin back through the hatch, I regretted that. But the following evening, I got the same tin back with the messages unchanged. This time I scratched lines through it all.

In the night, I tapped on the wall,

"No more guilt or forgive or mistake stuff. We will stick together. We cant do more than that."

"So be it."

58

The summer of that year became nothing but radiantly sunny days. The prison courtyard, always empty now, was black with dust. The air danced in the heavy sunlight between those walls. It stank in my cell.

We were not miserable. We had a sense of being together and of purpose. We sensed a growing tension among "them." We talked about that for hours, now especially during the night, when we could not sleep and it was easier to hear the taps on the stone. Was something brewing in Bosnia among our people? Every day one of us had his chains taken off and was led in front of the Investigating Judge. I never saw anyone on the way to his room in the infantry barracks, but the corridors were more and more cluttered with boxes, saddles, cartridge belts and even rifles just stacked about unguarded. I didn't feel locked out from the world as I had expected. The world now was here, where we were.

The food trustee gave out an occasional scrap of paper to wipe yourself with (we each had a bucket in our cell by way of toilet), and one day he gave me the front page of the *Neue Freie Presse*, a Vienna newspaper. I'm sure he did it intentionally. Here were suddenly almost two pages of news, printed less than a week ago. Almost, for the bottom of the front page was taken up with what was called a "feuilleton," a sloppy biography of a Renaissance nobleman called Gardeno—only in prison would you read this to the end. And on page 2 were advertisements for summer resorts on the North Sea and in the mountains, for garden concerts, chauffeurs' umbrellas, and for the twice-weekly express train, Saint Petersburg–Vienna–Cannes on the Mediterranean. Tuesdays and Saturdays, first class only. I read those ads first, every syllable. I puzzled over the express train timetable as if I were about to take it. I was afraid to start on the news items.

Most of them, though, were from the same catchment basin

as the express train and the chauffeurs' umbrellas. Prince Konrad, whoever he was, Princess Gisela von Bogun, and their suite had arrived from Hohenschwangau Castle, at Hotel Seespitz in Plansee and taken tea on the terrace. A burglary in the jewelry shop of Ludwig Klaus in Vienna had netted 2,000 crowns. There were three cases of rabies in Vienna, and two waiters, both twenty-six years old, had almost drowned while bathing in the Danube. The Rabbi Dr. Funk had been flung off the rear balcony of a Vienna streetcar in a curve and been treated for cuts in his lower lip. The cattle year market in Hungarian-Hradish would be held on July 20 and 21. In Triest, "Santos good average" coffee was sold for 56 crowns— it didn't say for what quantity. Coffee men would know. An American dollar that day was worth 4.95¾ crowns. Eugenie, the widow of Napoleon III, had been warned by a Paris police- man in the Tuileries for picking a flower, a forget-me-not she put in her prayer book. She had promised not to do it again, and the reporter showed he was deeply aware of the tragedy and irony of it all. There were examination results, and a deputy had been raised to the nobility. Then a political column in which, buried amidst elaborate sentences on the theory of international law, I came upon the words, "the Belgrade Gov- ernment conspiracy." That was us. And the essay went on to ask, "Who paid for this? Bombs are expensive. The engineers who make them have high salaries." There it stopped, to be continued on an inside page I would never get to see. Then another news item: the paper had telephoned the Serbian legation in Vienna. A *Diener* (valet? servant?) had answered the phone and told the reporter no one of the staff came in during the afternoon. Which hadn't stopped the *Neue Freie Presse* from asking why the legation had the Serbian flag fly- ing, thereby exasperating the burghers of Vienna. Well, he didn't know, the servant had said. There was a small black ribbon attached to it, but the paper reported you couldn't see that from the street.

In that sea of summer-hotel ads and tea-taking princes, the government-conspiracy bit and the phone call about the flag were well-nigh lost. At first sight. The more I looked at the paper, the more they seemed to throw an ominous light on all that placid comment. But perhaps it was simply that you weren't meant to peruse it that slowly and carefully and in a Sarajevo military prison, instead of a Vienna café.

Judge Pfeffer: "State the name of the organization in Belgrade that put you up to this. Name their officers."

I had seen him pace around and knew now that he was short, shorter than I, fat, and quickly out of breath. He had a thick pillow in his desk chair, which did not make him look taller but more like a child sitting at the dining table with the grown-ups. He seemed paler each time I saw him, as if he were locked up, too, between interrogations.

"Answer the judge." This from a gendarme.

The judge looked annoyed at him. He didn't need help from the lowly.

"Who put you up to this?"

"I've already answered several times. No one."

Judge Pfeffer: "Do you really expect us to believe that some Bosnian schoolboys would dare an attempt against the Heir Apparent without being made to do this?"

"No—I admit that is not the most truthful answer. I was put up to this. By you."

"By me?"

"By the Empire, Your Honor."

Judge Pfeffer slowly lifted his head until he looked at the ceiling. It was his way of indicating that I should be taken away.

I thought of Milan with his Serbian pebble against the bedroom window of the Emperor. Rulers and foreign agitators always go together. How else could Franjo Josip believe his own crap about being Father of his nations.

"Wait," Pfeffer said.

We all turned and looked at him. One gendarme let go of my arm and scratched himself. "If this was your own plan, Princip, then you are criminals who have to be destroyed; but if you convince us that ruthless adventurers in Belgrade got you into this, we must consider you as nothing more than young boys led astray. Think about that."

I thought about Franjo Josip. How had he received the

news? Wouldn't an old man unavoidably have felt a twinge of triumph at surviving his nephew who had so visibly prepared himself to be his successor, once he was dead?

More, could that bigoted man have resisted seeing the hand of God in it all? Wasn't it the Almighty himself who like a cosmic protocol officer had used this humble tool, a Bosnian peasant's son, to eliminate the satrap and his Stuttgart countess, thus assuring the purity of the Habsburg line and without any fiddling with the principle of legitimacy? Who else but God could have solved his problem so flawlessly?

"Have you considered?" the judge asked.

"Are you sure, sir, that the Emperor shares your feelings in the matter?"

"Is that all you have to say to me?"

I said, "Can I have a visit?"

"No."

"Can I write one letter?"

He shook his head, and they led me out of his room.

59

In the absolute night without a glimmer that came not long before dawn, I had fallen asleep, when there were loud, dull bangs on my wall. Heaven knows what Cabri was using; his head maybe. He would if necessary, I was sure. Five short, one long; one short, one long; four short, two long. On and on, until it penetrated to me what he was signaling.

WAR

It had been light for hours when the bread cart finally came. The trustee was alone; no guard's eye watched me through the judas hole. His grin was there as always and he gave me two pieces of bread instead of one. He kept the hatch open.

"I know," I whispered.

"They're bombarding Belgrade," he said, not even lowering his voice. "The Empire has declared war on Serbia and they gave you as the reason. How about that?"

His grin widened. I stared at him.

"Don't worry my boy," he went on. "They were spoiling for it. Only yesterday, the corporal said to me, 'Serbia has caved in. It's given in to all our demands.' Well now, it shows they wanted their war, anyway, doesn't it. Just let them, just wait."

Bombarding Belgrade. That Austrian gunboat I had seen steam by with its steel turret and the old Kalemegdan fortress with the Turkish brass cannon that kids used to sit on.

"Don't worry, my boy," the trustee said again. "They're in for some surprises, our lords and masters."

He must have heard someone. He said, "Eat that bread quick," and banged the hatch close.

There had been wild moments in Belgrade when we said we would spark an uprising in Bosnia. I don't think any of us had really believed it in his heart; but that was, in Cabri's words, a "So what" consideration. You could only hope.

On our green walk into Bosnia, Trifko and I had both felt as if we were carrying that spark in the hollow of our hands straight to Sarajevo. But that, too, was like a dream, where you know you are dreaming. You wouldn't have dared admit even to yourself that it could be more than that.

Now the opposite had happened.

The rulers, as always, would answer each shot with thousands.

Your Honors, the desperate violence of the people is answered a thousandfold by you.

A judge is reading his mail. A journalist from Vienna, if there'd be one, draws a dog and a cat on his note pad. Violence of the people? Are you talking about yourself, accused, shooting off a pistol? Yes, Your Honor. I apologize for not being more modest and diffident. I apologize for using words found in badly mimeographed pamphlets. I apologize for boring you. I would love to tell you of our secret weekly rendezvous in Belgrade nightclubs with wads of bank notes changing hands.

Then you could contentedly feel everyone is really the same.

60

The Emperor wasn't grieving for his nephew. Or even if he were. Empires do not start wars emotionally any more. The Germans push east and want all Poles dead. The Austrians push south and want us dead. I knew all that. Perhaps we had salved the pride of us the victims by not waiting but striking the initial blow.

I calmed down.

For the first time I began to think fiercely about escape. Now it was awful to be put away like this, now it seemed meaningful that the cyanide had not killed us.

I tapped on the wall, "We must be out there and not in a cell."

Cabri answered, "But we fired the first shots." And after a pause, "And threw the first grenade."

That was not the answer I had wanted.

A new, icy fear. Finally I managed to signal, "Maybe we helped Austria. A cruel irony question mark."

There was no answer, even when I kicked the wall. Cabri must have been at the other end of his cell. He came back to me with, "No. We all say no. Stop doubting yourself. The world knows. Russia. We are no longer alone."

We stayed silent after that for the rest of the day. I was in a daze. I didn't even reason much. I sat on the floor and watched the movements of the shadows across the stone. I conjured up images of war in them, but all I knew were images of the Balkan wars, of cavalry charging, of men climbing along mountain paths with their rifles. This was different. The Empire had machines, machine guns, trucks, motors. Beside it were the fearful guns from its ally Germany, reported to fire over miles and to destroy towns beyond the horizon.

The last line of shadow spread out into grayness. The sun set.

I tried to imagine those guns being ferried across the Danube and across the Sava. It was hard to see except when you imagined hundreds of men with ropes, as in a drawing in our school history book of slaves building the Pyramids. Perhaps they'd find that in 1914 those men wouldn't be slaves any longer; perhaps they'd refuse to pull those guns in position to destroy the men and women across the rivers.

I stood in a dark square surrounded by torchlight. I told them to drop the ropes from their hands and to turn the barrels of those guns on the castles of their officers. I saw their faces lifted up at me, puzzled, undecided.

Nothing was heard in the square but the soughing of the wind and the soft hiss of torches.

61

War. Everything was political and general and totally impersonal. Incomprehensible.

It had been a Monday or Tuesday that the trustee told me about the bombardment of Belgrade. The morning after, the guard was back and we learned nothing more. But when Sunday came, a chaplain made the round of the cells. That hadn't happened before.

I heard a man go into Cabri's cell and come out again a moment later. Then they opened my door and I saw the priest. I was going to receive him better than Cabri had.

He did not look priestly, just an ordinary man, a Serb even, I thought.

We exchanged greetings, and he told me that I had to pray for the Empire now, to atone for my deed.

I said, why? Was the Empire in danger?

A fishy look. "It needs God's help, as always."

"I'd think that Austria and Germany can defeat Serbia without the need of divine help." I tried to smile when I said that, but I was too late. I had done it. He was already up and knocked on the hatch to be let out.

"There is a rebellious spirit in you, too," he said, "which will be fatal to boys in your position." He sounded hard but there was something nervous in his manner.

I stuck to my smile. "Why pray for the Empire? Is Russia in the war?"

He turned his back to me, impatiently waiting for the guard to open the door for him. Without looking around, he said, "Yes. The Austrian and German Empires are now at war with Russia. And with France and with England. Pray for forgiveness."

The iron on iron of the door closing, *clang*—through my brain and through my body.

Forgiveness! I don't need forgiveness. We are swept away, forgotten already. No one remembers Sarajevo. Pathetic broodings on the right to violence. Empires are at war against one another.

I asked Judge Pfeffer, "Your Honor, why don't you have us shot and have done with it?"

I wasn't trying to be foolhardy or gallant. That was a genuine question. I had not expected I'd be brought to that room again.

What more could they want of us? Could a pistol shot be worth discussing when a million men started firing at each other? Weren't they too busy now?

The judge shuffled his papers and then lifted his head and eyed me in a way I had not seen before. A deadly look. I froze.

"Don't concern yourself with it, Princip," he said. "Be assured that you will die in the manner, and at the time, suited to the needs and the laws of this Empire."

I was going to challenge that; I was going to ask him, how did he know those laws and needs were not in conflict, what precisely was an Investigating Judge meant to investigate. But I didn't open my mouth.

I had once seen him smile. I had imagined that he had begun to understand us somewhat and to look at us as fellow beings. I had overlooked that they always cheat.

62

A Monday morning. The trustee with the grin had long vanished. The bread was now handed out by a silent old man. He muttered something to me but I didn't hear what.

The gendarmes came and took me to Judge Pfeffer's room. As the door opened, I first saw the judge's chair, empty, then the back of a boy standing there with a gendarme next to him. He was Trifko.

We fell into each other's arms. The gendarmes didn't seem to care and said nothing. Then Cabri was brought in, and then Danilo. A room full of police and the four of us in the middle.

No one knew what to say. We just smiled and went on shaking our hands and patting each other on the shoulders.

"You all look pretty good," Cabri said.

"You, too. You haven't changed."

Then a new silence. And yesterday he and I had spent hours tapping out what we now could have said in a few minutes.

"Silence," a gendarme shouted needlessly. Judge Pfeffer came in and sat down at his desk. His clerk followed him.

"I will now read to you," Pfeffer started, "a formal indictment drawn up by the District Court of Sarajevo for premeditated murder, conspiracy to murder, and high treason, against the accused, Gavrilo Princip, Nedeljiko Cabrinovic. . . ."

We didn't listen. We just looked at each other, some of us with tears.

I felt so glad that I thought: this is such an unexpected extra thing that's happening to me, I swear I'll call myself fortunate now, no matter what'll happen to me after this.

Hands and faces of friends instead of stone. Beings who knew what I knew, who were, with me, part of a general plan of nature, of a kind of belief or at least hope, for a hidden generosity in the world. Pfeffer and I were no fellow creatures. I would rather talk through stone walls than look at Pfeffers.

He and his people were—oh, to hell with him and his people. To hell! Danilo, Trifko, Cabri—how can I use this short moment adequately to show my love and loyalty and my happiness for the way you are?

Danilo whispered, "I just got this from my neighbor who is a soldier. Austria's cleared out of Belgrade. The Serbian army —" he waited and looked from one to the other "—the Serbian army has crossed the Sava and the Drina."

"Jesus!" Cabri cried and Trifko jumped to look over the heads of the gendarmes out of the window, as if he expected to see that army come marching down the road. And I put my arms around Danilo and we hugged each other with all our strength. No German monster guns. Our people crossing our rivers.

"You are behaving like small boys," Judge Pfeffer said, unaccountably accepting all this. "You would have done better to listen to the indictment."

No one reacted and that seemed to disconcert him. He looked ill at ease at the gendarmes, probably feeling foolish. I was sorry for him and said, "We know what it says, sir. But we haven't seen each other for so long."

He shrugged. "You have the right under law to protest the indictment," he mumbled, "but I don't advise—"

"I want to," Cabri immediately said to him.

"Why?"

"The war goes on—who knows what will happen next," Cabri answered with a smile.

Then Pfeffer had that same deadly look I had seen on him before. "Do you think maybe that you'll be acquitted?" he asked. "Before the war is over, we'll have hanged a dozen Cabrinovics."

He had fooled me just this once more. I turned my back to him; I wanted to see my friends. I never again looked him in his face.

And Cabri answered very coolly, "So much the worse for the hangmen of the Empire."

Two other civilians came in and stood and whispered with Judge Pfeffer. The gendarmes yawned and picked their teeth. It was certainly an unusual occasion.

"Listen, all of you, let's not act humble at the trial," I said. "Please believe me there's no point to it. They've made up their minds. We must speak out."

Cabri nodded; Trifko was going to say something, but Pfeffer looked over his shoulder and ordered, "Take them back to their cells." And to the clerk, "Give each man a copy of the indictment."

Danilo said loudly, "Yes, the Sava and the Drina."

As soon as I was back, Cabri started wall tapping, "Read that indictment. It is full of God. They should let us out and lock up God." I sat on the floor and read, "It was the will of the Almighty that on June 28 of this year . . . the Almighty saved his Imperial and Royal Highness Francis Ferdinand by not permitting the bomb to explode in his automobile. . . . the Almighty willed the bullet to hit his Imperial and Royal Highness Francis Ferdinand. . . ." and on and on. "Stupid," I answered, but Cabri was really worked up about it, and he went on for a long time tapping, "Arrest God. Arrest God. Let us out."

It taught us that they did listen in to us. An hour later a guard came by and took all the indictments away again.

The following day they brought us other ones, the same statement but this time without God.

63

It was already after the evening soup when the door of my cell was unlocked, and a man was standing there, round face, youngish, gray suit, felt hat in his hand.

"I am Doktor Feldbauer," he said. "I am the appointed lawyer for you and three of the others."

"Three of the others? We are only four," I answered, getting to my feet.

Feldbauer almost-smiled. "There have been twenty-five arrests so far."

"My line of defense for you," he immediately went on, "will be that you did not initiate your act, that you are a confused young man and a dupe of propaganda from Serbia."

I pulled myself together. I said, "I don't want you to follow that line of defense. It is not true. I want to explain my deed at the trial."

"I did not come to ask you what you wanted," he answered. "I will see you at the trial." He knocked to be let out.

I sat down on the floor again. Good-bye, Feldbauer.

The guard opened the door for him and looked at us with a certain curiosity.

"By the way," Feldbauer said, "don't see yourself too soon as a Serbian martyr. You're not of age. Under the laws of the Empire you cannot receive the death penalty." He looked at the guard and repeated, "Yes, they can't hang him."

The guard shrugged. "Socialists," he said. "We'll get them some other way."

No death penalty when you are under age. I had not known. Nor would it ever have mattered. We had ourselves decided our fate, we thought.

But how weird to be now so enmeshed in this machine that they couldn't hang me any more, while every Serb outside this prison depended for his life on luck or the whim of the nearest Austrian or Hungarian officer. Who'd report a peasant strung up from his plum tree by an Austrian infantry platoon? Europe—that's to say, ten newspaper correspondents—must be aware of us in here, be we four or twenty-five, as it didn't bother to be aware of our millions out in the towns and villages and mountains.

Could it be that the four of us—no, not four. Danilo was of age, he was twenty-three—

Could it be that they wanted us alive anyway, to use us, to issue phony confessions and depict us as pawns in an international plot? Was that what Pfeffer had meant? But we were still in Bosnia. Our friends were outside those walls and in the streets of Sarajevo. They couldn't silence us that well without killing us.

I fell asleep although it was not even quite dark yet. For once I did not dream, and when I woke up, in pitch-dark, it took me a moment to realize where I was. Even who I was.

Then I lay there as alone, as bare to the world, as I had not been since the days I had discovered my real ideas and friends. I couldn't focus on war or anything, only on myself. Half fearful, half numbed. I asked myself, could it be that I would survive after all, survive while Djula, or the boss of the Cornerbar, or that boy who believed in "realistic tactics, and day-to-day work" would fight and die? Did I want to? Was it better to live the rest of your life in jail? I tried without cheating to really imagine the door opening and men entering the cell to take me to my execution. First that frightened me, paralyzed me. Then I got outside my little shell of self again, conjured up the Serbian army crossing the rivers into Bosnia, and found courage in that. Then I thought, how terrible to die before knowing what will happen. What does courage mean, and sacrifice? Putting so much of yourself outside yourself that you can die in peace? I wrapped myself in my blanket and thought, I am saved. And was ashamed. No door opened. No one came to hang me.

If you really want to, you can always kill yourself. I knew I could.

No one came to tell me that I still had that duty.

I did not know.

64

We sat with our arms crossed as they had commanded us to, on the front bench of a room in the military prison. They put me in the middle; there were five of us. The fifth man was Veljiko, the teacher from Priboj village who had helped us during the magic walk. It took me a moment to recognize him.

It was a blow that he was there.

And so was the presence of Misko, the gentleman from the Tuzla reading room who had kept the arms for me, and who was sitting behind us, and of the peasant guides of that walk, and of students from Sarajevo and men I did not know. As Feldbauer had announced, we were twenty-five in all.

We had no chance to talk in the courtroom, not a whisper. I studied the faces of those two men, the teacher and that extraordinary banker, who had been swept into this through us. They had made a bitter sacrifice, unlike ours, for they didn't believe in rebellion. Yet they simply stated why they had helped and nothing more. When they caught my eyes on them, they both nodded reassuringly.

They, and Danilo, were the only men of age, who could be condemned to death, and knew they would. The guides would be saved by Trifko's and my insistence that they had acted under threat.

None of these men should have been there and it was monstrous that they were. Our conspiracy had not been thought out beyond the faulty bottle of cyanide, and those along the way had been unprepared for Austria's determination to ferret out everything that might be turned into proof pointing at Belgrade, and they had acted as if this were still the innocent year 1389 of Kosovo.

The room wasn't what you would imagine for a trial. It was not a real courtroom but the officers' mess of the prison or some such place. It was small, with rows of benches, striped wallpaper, oil lamps hanging from the ceiling, a big window in the back and one behind the judges' table. It had wainscoting of brown wood, turned nearly black, framed pictures on the walls, and even a bookrack with books and illustrated magazines that hadn't been removed. We sat there for ten days and sometimes I thought, this setting will of a sudden win out and make the presiding judge close his dossier and say, "Let us talk of what this is really about."

There were three judges (no Pfeffer), a prosecutor (the father of Maxim who had walked me past all those detectives), defense lawyers, clerks. In the back sat some more civilians, journalists it appeared, and a Jesuit priest. No friends, of course, no public. On each side of the row of benches stood half a dozen soldiers with rifle and bayonet.

Those judges and lawyers weren't all Austrians; the presiding judge had an Italian name, which I heard once but forgot; German and Serbian were both used in many accents. But everyone said what you would have thought they'd say; they were all part of the state and their actions and words were as precise and predictable as the movements in a classic ballet. That's what it was, a ballet, an Imperial ceremony. We were the only dissonants, or tried to be.

We and one unique lawyer. He was defending the teacher, and he first tried to read out a passage from *A History of the Slav Peoples*, which they wouldn't let him do, and he then stated that, Bosnia not legally having become part of the empire, Bosnians couldn't now be accused of high treason. A startled silence in the court. He was warned, and later put under accusation himself. The other lawyers behaved. One even apologized for being there and quoted Cicero, that defending a traitor would make him an accomplice.

Thus we defended ourselves. Not all in the same way, though as you'd have expected, it made no difference in the sentences. It wasn't in that hope that Danilo said he didn't believe in violence. He said it because it was true. As for me, I tried to find strength by wrapping myself into a kind of conscious contempt. It was hard to seem rude to men who seemed civilized. But we weren't talking to our judges, or to those Austrian journalists; it wasn't for them that we tapped out long deliberations about what to say through our walls in the night. We were talking to Sarajevo.

They let us speak because Sarajevo couldn't hear us. But there were clerks in that room who wrote down every word said. And the Empire finds it difficult if not impossible to destroy any official piece of paper.

Let them lock those words away twice over in the dustiest vault in Vienna; as long as they are not destroyed, they will one day out. For one day the Empire will fall.

The summer had ended. There were still days that turned sunny, but the strip of sky I could see above the judges' heads remained pale. In the mornings, the light started so gray and hesitant that I couldn't distinguish the faces of the soldiers who came to my cell to get me. We shuffled through dark corridors and when we were brought into the courtroom, a soldier lit the oil lamps.

Then it was just like my old Sarajevo schoolroom there on an October or November morning.

I was sitting on a school bench, with some of my grade school classmates still beside me.

Not much time had passed since then.

The oil lamp right above us threw long shadows over our faces, which were very white now and covered with stubble or beard. They'd cut our hair, but they didn't let us shave.

We wore our own suits and shirts, without the ties. Trifko was the only one of us four who somehow looked clean and not like a poor tramp.

65

Rebellion is not a suppression of measure in human affairs. Rebellion represents measure. It is the State, which never knows measure.

After a while, the soldier would blow the oil lamps out again. Then the judges' faces would be in the shade and hard to see, and the light from the gray or pale blue sky behind them would fall on us and show us for the haggard bunch we were.

We were asked with irony who had appointed us to speak for the people. Cabri said joint suffering had appointed us. I said perhaps I could speak for my six dead brothers and sisters buried in Grahovo. One human death weighed as much as any other. Why had there been no trial for those children's deaths? Cabri said, we didn't think in terms of leadership but of love for our fellow men.

"You talk about love for your fellow man and you kill?"

"It's a paradox we tried to solve by swallowing poison."

"Why do you think we are on earth?" he was asked.

"Not to pursue individual happiness. Not to serve the State either. But to become new men and women in a new anarchism."

The prosecutor said, "You admit then to being an anarchist?"

"Yes. But you do not know what the word means."

"Well, enlighten us. It would seem to mean that you are free to throw bombs and shoot off pistols."

"Not free to. It is our duty, to kill our tyrants."

"And you decide who those tyrants are?"

"No, the people. Read Locke."

"Ah, Locke—and did Mr. Locke ever shoot anybody?"

Another time I remember is when the presiding judge interrupted Trifko speaking about suppression. He asked him to explain, then, why thousands of loyal Slavs had volunteered for the front, and why the business community of Sarajevo had collected ten thousand gold crowns for a monument to the Heir Apparent. Trifko answered that businessmen in all countries were the same, that money does not smell, has no shame, cannot cry. Cabri smiled as he listened; I guessed those words must have come from him. "As for Slav soldiers in your army," Trifko went on, "if they are there, they can't be anything but an unconscious mass." The prosecutor jumped up and said he would file a new and separate indictment against Trifko for that treacherous statement.

Long, gray hours. Seas of mechanized words.

The order on earth, as it existed, was God's will. I asked if I were permitted then to see God's will in an automobile backing up to right in front of my pistol.

An echo of indignant murmurs. It didn't scare me.

The presiding judge, calmly: "The chauffeur had made a mistake in the route." "Princip," he now muttered as if just learning my name. He looked in his papers. "I see you stated that you are an atheist?"

I said yes.

Then how could I speak about love for mankind? Didn't I live in a materialistic world, in which all impulses were economical, or maybe chemical? Didn't I reject the fine impulses from the Christian and, eh (looking around), other faiths?

148

I threw a glance at Cabri on my side. We had talked about this in the night. It was like a well-prepared question at an exam. I thought of my winter in Grahovo Valley, and then, finally of my father. I was pleased because I knew exactly what I was going to say. "If I believed in your God, I wouldn't have been moved to desperate acts by being in your world. For then I'd know that the day will come when we'll all be comforted and justice done.

"But I believe we are blindly wandering in a silent universe. And therefore we need our fellow men's love, and need human justice on earth, now."

The judge did not answer and he leafed through the dossiers. It had become very dark outside, and I kept my eyes on the black clouds rather than on him. There was no sound except for a man coughing in the back. I am a tiny spot in a silent circular vastness.

The judge said, "All those accused who feel sorry for their deeds, stand up."

He asked me why I did not stand up.

I said I had done what I had meant to do. Except for the death of the Duchess of Hohenberg. Perhaps she, by being in Sarajevo, had been a victim of the same lie that we all were. Before I had finished those words, my friends had sat down again, too.

66

Five days of silence. We waited and talked. The hours flowed by, because we tried to hold on to them. Now we felt time running out on us. I'd wake up in the dark in a panic, and hastily tap out, "Cabri. Are you asleep," or something like that. He did the same.

Then the soldiers came back for us. This time they lined us up in the corridor, and the guard who took off our chains put on other ones that linked us in pairs. I had Trifko. We made no jokes about it.

We shuffled through the corridor and back into the court-room. The benches had gone. It was another dark morning but the lamps were not lit.

We stood there a long time until the judges came in. They sat down. The presiding judge put a black cap on his head. He opened a leather map and read out in a soft, even voice that he condemned Danilo, Veljiko the teacher, and the Tuzla banker to death by hanging.

They made no sound. These men had not meant to die. They had not even thought the plan was good.

As for us three, Cabri, Trifko, and I, who had meant to kill the satrap and ourselves, we were now told formally that we were too young to be hanged.

"I sentence each one of you," the judge read, "to twenty years of solitary imprisonment, in regulation chains. And you, Gavrilo Princip, will spend one day each month, and each June the twenty-eighth, in a darkened cell without food or water."

Then he read off lesser prison sentences for some of the others. And he acquitted the peasants; he had believed us about them.

A very short time later we were back in our cells. My bread and coffee were still sitting on the floor as I had left them when the soldiers came in. The coffee was still lukewarmish.

67

Weeks went by. Nothing changed. It rained and rained, and the courtyard looked like a marsh. I stood at my window for hours; I'd found a trick to rest my chains on a brick that stuck out. Rarely you'd see a soldier or a trustee go by, ducking closely to the wall and with his coat over his head.

I was sitting on my cot (they didn't bother me any more about hooking it up to the wall), conducting a conversation with Cabri, when my cell door was unlocked. Two soldiers came in and took me to a guard room, leaving on my irons. They told me to sit on a bench there and wait. It was warm, a stove was roaring. A minute later Trifko and Cabri were brought in. "This is it," we said.

Men came and went to warm and dry themselves and to bring new wood for the stove. Every one of them gave us a good stare. We sat quietly beside each other and soaked up the heat.

It got dark. A sergeant showed up and said to our two soldiers, who were busy playing cards, "Take them back to their cells."

"What's going on?" we asked.

"Don't worry about it, you've all the time in the world," he said with a sort of hiccup laugh.

We got up obediently. "Tomorrow," he said.

In the corridor, we asked the two if they knew where we'd be taken, but they didn't answer.

I was back at my window and stared at the Sarajevo sky. It was slightly tinted, reflecting the lights of the unseen town. A myriadth part of that reddish light was from the lamp behind Sophia's window. A thought from a French novel hero, stop it. The last evening. The last night. Our last night in Sarajevo. I had a feeling I almost loved my cell now.

The following morning I swallowed my bread and coffee and used the toilet bucket in great haste. But no one came. The day passed. We just tapped out single words, "Damn," "Hurrah," "Bosnia." My blood was beating in my temples. The courtyard lay dark and deserted.

The door was opened and the same soldiers led us, all three together this time, to that guard room.

We sat down again. "They're going to do this every day now," Cabri said, "to give us a chance to get nice and warm."

Four men entered, soldiers or gendarmes, in black uniforms I'd never seen before. One was a sergeant. He saluted our guardroom sergeant and said in German, "Sergeant Gunter. Prisoners' escort party." He didn't look at us.

"Right," our sergeant said. "May I see your documents?"

They handed papers back and forth. Both sergeants signed for us with a stub of pencil.

"Prisoners," Gunter now said in bad Serbian, to no one in particular, "get ready."

"Where are we going?" we asked.

He focused on us. "A long way." I thought he looked ill at ease rather than nasty.

"What about our things?" Trifko asked the guard sergeant.

"You won't need them. They'll be kept for you."

We stood up. Gunter and his three men fell in around us. "Wait!" our sergeant cried. "My chains. You can't take away my chains."

Gunter rubbed his chin. "We didn't bring any," he answered.

"Better take us back to our cells," Cabri said aloud.

"I can write out a receipt for them," Gunter suggested. The guard sergeant hesitated and then answered, "Well, alright." He gave Gunter the key.

Backed up almost against the door stood a closed army van with two horses, the kind they use for bread, or for wounded men. They made us climb into the back with the three soldiers, and closed the flap. A lamp hung from the ceiling and threw a murky light on us all.

We rattled down the hillside and made several turns. "We're crossing a bridge," I said, "I bet you we're on Skenderija." "No, we're not," Cabri answered. "Yes, we are."

One of the soldiers, without a word, lifted the flap.

Sarajevo. Bosna Serai.

A muddy street. I didn't know which one. Houses, lit windows. At a deserted crossroads, an electric lamp swinging from a wire. It had stopped raining, but you could hear water dripping everywhere.

Another turn. Better pavement, more lights. We passed a girl walking along under an umbrella. I saw her come home at the end of a day, a warm vestibule, the wet cloth of her coat against my skin as I kissed her. "Good-bye," I said soundlessly. A tree-lined street now; the wheels ran softly on the carpet of dead leaves.

The soldier looked at us, sighed, and let the flap drop back in place.

When the van came to a stop, we were in a freight yard of the railway station. We were hustled through a door onto an empty platform and into the last coach of a train sitting there.

It was an old wooden coach but with a through corridor as long-distance trains have. It had a feeble gas lamp and signs in four languages, advising on the danger of leaning out of the windows, and forbidding to spit. Gunter placed a soldier in each window seat, Cabri and Trifko on one side, and me facing them on the opposite bench. Large iron eyes had been screwed into the bottom of the benches and our ankle chains now were unlocked, led through those eyes, and locked again. Then Gunter pulled the greasy sailcloth blinds down on all the windows and on the door to the corridor, and he and the third soldier got off.

We sat. It got busy on the platform, voices and running steps. We could hear men thump into the compartment next to ours. Our two soldiers rolled cigarettes. They gave us one. The only cigarette I ever smoked. Outside, commands were shouted in German. The handle of our door moved, and our soldiers motioned to us to get rid of our cigarettes.

Gunter got back on with his other soldier. He raised a blind, and we saw a motley crowd of army personnel hurrying along the platform looking for empty places. Doors slammed, a whistle blew. Gunter carefully lowered the blind again and went out into the corridor.

We were moving.

There was a rip in one of the blinds. I could see a line of light through it. The line got broken more and more often, then it remained dark. Just once, one of the soldiers had a look out.

A dark countryside, with far off the yellow square of a lit farm window.

The train whistles again. At the farm, they may listen and wonder.

The blind is back in place.

68

Sergeant Gunter came back in, sat in the corner near the corridor, crossed his legs, lit a cigarette, and said to me, "General Potiorek is back in Belgrade."

I made a face. "We'll come out of this war," I answered. "And as one nation."

"We?"

"The Serbs, Croats—all of us. The South Slavs."

He looked thoughtful rather than annoyed. "You think so, eh? Well— And you don't mind leaving your carcass in some prison grave?"

I smiled and waved my hand.

"We counted on that," Cabri said. "Where're we going?"

"You'll find out."

Nothing further was said to us. The two men at the windows slept. Gunter smoked. The fourth soldier was away. We sat very still. No one had forbidden us to talk, but we said nothing. At one point, Cabri shook hands with me, and then with Trifko. Every now and again we'd do that again, just touching hands.

I slept. When I opened my eyes, there were edges of light along the blinds. The train had come to a halt. Only Gunter and one soldier were there, eating bread and ham. "I have to piss," I said.

"One at a time."

We were taken to the toilet on the train. From the corridor window, I saw a plain of brownish grass, flat as a pancake, under thick rolls of morning fog. It looked far, alien, German. Invisible birds were flying around in that fog and uttering painful cries.

I stood still and asked my soldier, "Where are we?" He shrugged, and muttered, "Kreuz. Slovania." "Fuck it," I said, "we're out of Bosnia already. Oh, dammit." He half-smiled and shrugged again. He was the man who had lifted the flap of the van for us. I wondered where he was from; he was not a Serb. I smiled back at him.

When we were all three chained to our seats, Gunter gave us bread and passed around a canteen with coffee.

The train started up again. We rolled along for hours. The four men took shifts in sitting with us. We dozed. Then another stop. After a long wait, we started backing up onto a siding. "Hurrah," Cabri said, "to Sarajevo!" Our soldier laughed. Then followed endless shunting, whistle signals, other trains rattling by. Gunter went out into the corridor to look. He came back and said meaningfully, "Much military traffic."

He left the corridor door open to air the compartment. It was dark again. I heard Trifko hum a song, but we didn't take it up. We slept.

When I woke, the train was going very fast. Everyone else was asleep. I studied the faces of my friends in the uncertain light. Cabri looked old and tired. Trifko looked like a sick child. I thought, I wish I could do something to protect them, to help them. I wasn't being heroic. Oddly, I had the feeling that I didn't mind for myself. Why? Perhaps because I had fired the shots.

Lights shone through the rip in the blind. The train slowed down in a series of uneasy lurches and finally stopped. Gunter opened his eyes, looked at his watch, and then out of the window. He unlocked our foot chains. "Everyone out," he ordered.

We stumbled onto a sparsely lit platform. We tried to loosen our arms and legs. No people, but bales and crates everywhere. On a white enamel sign, in blue the letters WIEN. "Holy shit," Cabri said, "we're in Vienna."

Gunter put us into a kind of formation, with a soldier next to each of us, and marched us through an underground passage and up a ramp. He seemed to know exactly where to go. Suddenly, we found ourselves on a bright platform crowded with people. A line of soldiers and police, and behind them a throng of men and women all looking at us. An enormous uproar began. "There they are," they shouted. "Filthy Serbs. Murderers. Shoot them out of hand. Shoot them. Mail 'em to the Czar, in pieces."

"What a vile trick," Cabri said. "Who set this up?"

"Silence!" Gunter screamed at him.

He didn't look very happy. He quick-marched us past them, while the soldiers and police pushed them back. I saw their faces, white and red with anger. Men in black overcoats with fur collars, shaking their fists, ladies in big hats, porters. Even children. A man in a cloth cap spat at us but he only hit a policeman on the shoulder. A housewife shouted at me, "Did the Jews pay you well for this?"

We came to a door marked, "Railway Police." Gunter led us into a small, empty room. "Two outside on guard," he ordered, "bayonets fixed." And to us, "Sit on the floor. No talking."

The shouting and screaming died out. Gunter left the room. After a while, a policeman came in and gave us bread and sausage.

We smiled at each other. "Fucking Schwaben." "We'll get them."

We were marched out again in the night. The platform was empty, most of the lights were dimmed. Papers and dirt blew about. The station clock said a quarter to three. I shivered.

We were taken to a train and put into a compartment exactly like the one before, the same blinds, the same iron eyes for our chains. "It's a remarkable Empire," Cabri muttered.

We still had Sergeant Gunter, but three new soldiers, Hungarian infantrymen, shabby-looking reservists. As soon as they sat down, they pulled out bread and pork, sprinkled it with paprika they carried in cones of newspaper, and started eating slowly, cutting off the pieces near their mouths with clasp knives. They ignored both us and the sergeant.

"Where are we going?" Cabri asked once more almost automatically.

"Theresienstadt." Gunter waited for our reaction, but we had never heard of it.

"It's a fortress on the Elbe River," he said. "Near the German border."

The German border. A thousand miles from our mountains, from the East. In the dark heart of Europe. I heard my friends swear under their breaths. The German fucking border.

It was such an endless wearisome ride. But I wished it would not end. "A fortress?" I asked Gunter.

"I guess it's only a prison now. A military prison. For deserters. And people like you."

"Who are people like us?"

Gunter looked almost shy. He shrugged and lit another cigarette.

69

It was twilight once more, twilight of an early winter evening, when Gunter raised the blinds. The train had halted. "This is it," he said. "Everyone out."

A talus of cinders along the railway track. Holding up our shackles, we stamped our feet. Rain mixed with sleet was drizzling down. Ahead of us, the last passenger of our train, a soldier on crutches, vanished into a wooden station building. One lamppost lit up the name THERESIENSTADT on the wall. It was painted in black, in Gothic letters, hooked verticals like a name in a medieval manuscript. The three Hungarian infantrymen, bayonet on rifle, stood facing us, chewing, with blank eyes, as they had been all day. Gunter had gone to look for someone or something.

Here and there a lamp blinked in the thickening darkness.

On one side of the track were fields; on our side stood two huge halls, abandoned factories, I thought. Most of their windows were broken, and the shattered panes reflected some last scraps of light from the overcast sky.

Gunter came back alone, holding a sheet of paper. He gathered up his gear and called, "Prisoners and escort, march."

We went around the wooden building, stumbling on stones and rails with our numb legs. Gunter did not try to make us go faster than we could.

We walked down an empty, black asphalt road, chains dragging along the ground. Only in its puddles was some light still left. I tried to walk looking up at the sky. Store up sky. The road ended at a T-junction. One arm led to the town, such as it was: somber houses in nineteenth-century middle-European style with all sorts of turrets and crenelations stood along an avenue with electric light. The other arm of the junction led into darkness. Gunter looked at his paper and commanded, "Right turn." We continued into the darkness.

"Jesus, it is cold here," Trifko said.

"We've gone straight north for three days."

"Yes."

"Do you know where we are on the map?" he asked me.

"Sort of. On the road from Prague to Dresden, I think."

"That's right," Gunter said unexpectedly from the dark.

A high blind wall loomed up in front of us.

"Jesus," Trifko said again. His voice shook.

We crossed a wooden bridge. Lamps showed an inky moat underneath, in which all sorts of debris floated. A terrible smell rose from it.

A soldier stepped out from a sentry box and challenged Gunter halfheartedly. A gate opened. I tried to have one more look at the sky, but a lamp blinded me.

We stood in a stone room, the floor and walls and roof were all of enormous blocks of granite. It held only a couple of wooden benches and a light bulb dangling from the high ceiling. It was as cold and muted as in a tomb. "Sit down," Gunter said. The soldiers sat across from us, leaning on their rifles. Gunter vanished.

I saw that Trifko was trembling. I put my hand on his. He tried to smile. "I'm just very cold," he muttered.

Gunter reappeared with a corporal and some soldiers, who leaned against the wall, their rifle butts resting on the floor.

Gunter stood in front of us. He hesitated. I thought he was

going to shake hands with us. "Good luck," he said and left with the three Hungarians.

"Princip, Gavrilo," the corporal called. "You're first."

I stood up with difficulty.

"Good-bye." "Good-bye." "Good-bye." "Before twenty years." "When we've won the war."

I followed the corporal. I turned around when I got to the door. "Hurrah for us," Cabri called. I looked at them for the last time in my life.

The corporal gave me a slight push. I entered an office and the door shut behind me.

I stood at a desk where a sergeant was filling out papers. He was tired and old. His collar was open and the inside was black with grease.

"Princip, Gavrilo. Sign here."

I bent over and signed for myself.

He motioned with his head, and two soldiers took me by my arms through another door. A small, warm room, with a wooden floor and a stove. A young orderly got up from behind a table. "The key," he said to the soldiers. "One of you go get the key for his irons."

He looked in my mouth. "Any contagious diseases?" he asked.

I shook my head.

"Don't go and report sick here," he said in a friendly voice. "This is not a sanitarium. If you're still alive a year from now, you're cheating."

They took off my chains, and then the two soldiers got hold of my arms again and we entered a washroom, a row of sinks and taps along one wall. They told me to strip and wash. I put my clothes on a stool and hastily washed under a tap. They handed me a piece of sacking to dry myself with.

"You can stand on it," one of them said. The floor was wet and grimy. The other brought me an undershirt and underpants, socks, a striped prison uniform, a cap of brown canvas, and old army boots. I stood hopping around but I couldn't get them on. He went to a shelf and brought me a larger pair. There was no number on the uniform as they always had in the books we read. "Take your towel with you," they said. "Your own clothes stay here."

They marched me off through a long, narrow corridor, one granite block wide. Our steps echoed ahead and behind us. Every thirty feet or so was a light.

"There's never any food the first day. Never. It's the rule," they told me. They sounded as if they wanted to reassure me.

We descended a flight of steps into a basement.

We passed the barred door of a large empty casemate. More passageway, and then we stopped at an iron door with a little half-circle window with two bars making a cross. It was within a wall at least three feet thick, and I didn't see where it could lead to.

"We wait here," they said. One of them held on to my arm, to prevent me from falling, I think.

After a while a man appeared in a kind of blue overalls. He carried chains and keys. He scrutinized me, and then he put ankle and wrist chains on me. Regulation Habsburg chains of twenty-four pounds; they were so much heavier than the ones I had gotten used to, that I keeled over. The soldier held on to me and pulled me up.

The man in the overalls unlocked that door. "Your cell," he said. "Reveille at five. No talking. Never. To no one. Don't forget."

The door closed behind me. I was in a cell or better, a hollow within a wall. The light from the corridor showed a wooden bunk with a straw mattress and a folded blanket, a bucket, and a jug.

I lay down. I shook with cold and fear.

70

Time froze. I was flailing, slowly, in a morass of timelessness.

I was struggling against my body. Got up, had my foot chain led through the ring in the wall, put on my shoes, drank the barley coffee. Ate half the slice of bread and kept the other half till midday. Stood or sat with my blanket around me. Some guards didn't allow that; others did. The water in the jug was frozen in the morning, but later it often thawed out. I'd force myself to wash my face with a bit scooped from the surface. Deeper down in the jug floated an undefinable green slime. I'd dry on that towel. No newspaper here to wipe your behind nor soap: I quickly became repulsive, vile. No lice, though, it was too cold. They emptied the bucket when it was near overflowing and gave it back with quicklime in the bottom. Once a month they took me to the washroom to wash shivering under a tap, and then I'd get clean underwear. I didn't know that in advance; the guards were not allowed to speak to me. But I'd come to dread that ordeal. You'd have been better off left alone. Those first weeks I got a tin of soup in the evening with beans or mashed-up potatoes or rice in it, a lovely hot, sticky mass you could feel go down your petrified innards. They ended that later and gave two boiled potatoes or beets or turnips, cold, cold as everything else was. A nausea of cold. They wanted me dead and I wasn't going to comply. I didn't get used to the cold but I did get used to the hunger and dirt.

The earliest days I still said, "Yesterday at this time I was on a train," or "Last week, I was talking to Cabri." Eyes kept appearing behind the semicircular window, men who wanted to have a look at me. One link of my hand irons had a sharp point and with it I scratched reddish lines on the wall for every day gone by. But presently I let it go. The beat of life slowed down and near stopped. A minute lasted an hour, an hour a year.

It could not *be*. Life could not be like this. It was impossible. As if a brain in a bottle of alcohol in a laboratory were conscious. If limbo was like this, it was worse than hell. How easy for human beings to construct a limbo on earth. A dungeon, chains, a bunk and a bucket eternalize the minute before a man in pain faints into unconsciousness.

I got ill and that really helped because coughing spells and fever ate up time. Hours began to pass without a thought or a trace. Days and nights became a blur of darkness and half-light from the passageway, all enveloped in the icy moistness of the air, the floor, the walls, and even the straw mattress, which, when you lay down on it in the evening, was covered with a kind of greasy dew. If I thought in that period, I don't remember much of it.

The first clear event was the first time someone talked to me. I don't know when it was, two or three months after our arrival, perhaps. My fever had probably gone. A man in uniform, I couldn't see in the dim light what he was, came into my cell and read from a sheet of paper something like, "By order of the Military Command for Theresienstadt at Leitmeritz, I now inform you that three of your fellow conspirators have been executed by hanging, in accordance with the sentence of the Sarajevo District Court." And he read off the names of Danilo, the teacher, and the banker. Then he put the paper in a pocket and looked at me. I collected my thoughts, and said, "Please tell me how Cabri and Trifko are." He did not seem to understand. "The two who came here with me." But he left without answering.

That message might have been meant as a torture, or more likely it was in accord with the unfathomable rules of the military machine. What it did was stop me in my descent into a foggy madness. My thoughts started up again. I saw clear. I told myself to think in terms of duty.

These men had died because of us, me. Never mind our cyanide. They had died. Unwillingly. Danilo no longer existed. That once-in-eternity combination of thoughts, traits, hopes, love, sadness had been obliterated by a Sarajevo hangman who had cut off the oxygen needed to feed Danilo's body. Surrounded by the ocean of air, he had choked. I could say, "I'd rather be dead," easily because it was true, but I wasn't dead. I, Gavre, existed, registered dark and light. If the war ended tomorrow, I would learn about it. Danilo was destroyed. If the earth collided with the sun tomorrow, it would make no difference to him. In fact, there was nothing left to correspond to that "him" but our thoughts of Danilo. It was up to us.

I stopped, mostly, being afraid and sad for myself. I had the task of thinking about these men.

I knew next to nothing about the teacher and the man from

Tuzla. I conjured up their faces again and again, and repeated the few words we had spoken, in the Tuzla reading room and in the dark near Proboj in those wet fields. Danilo—with him I had years of talking, arguing, and learning things. But his face now was least clear of those three. I repeated their names like a Tibetan monk in prayer.

Now I was using time. Needing it. I turned to Trifko and Cabri. They were in this stone pile; I visualized it from the outside, a beehive of cells, looking like that Tower of Babel I had once seen in a medieval painting. Not a sound penetrated my walls; even when the guard entered, in the morning to chain me to the wall, in the evening to unlock me, I heard him only at the last moment when he turned the key. But they were near me; I believed in the power of thought to travel; if Trifko knew I was thinking of him, he would stop shaking.

I often knew one of them was thinking of me. It seemed simple then, understood. As obvious as that we hadn't changed our minds that day in the library. Bender Abbas, the wretched seaport. We were its last three inhabitants.

I knew Trifko hadn't been afraid to die, nor Cabri, nor myself. It's a kind of fearlessness that runs out, though. But with ten million men at war with one another, how would we have dared be afraid? Not dying, aloneness was our mortal enemy. We had to go on thinking of ourselves as "us."

I made it my duty to think about the satrap. To maintain the meaning of what we had done.

I stared at the cross of the bars in the door or, at night, into the darkness lying on me, and I could see his face, the bulging blue eyes, the wrinkled cylindrical uniform and the sun through the plumed hat.

He had been a human being, he had been born, he had been a child. I tried to think of him that way, because I wanted to understand and taste remorse. But I couldn't.

I scratched this sign on the wall with my chain:

That was Sarajevo. The straight line was Appel Quay, the bent line Francis Joseph Street. At the crossline was Schiller's door, where he and I met. Those three lines were a picture, a dusty quay, a glittering river, the scrawny trees, the child in the sailor suit waving. It became the magic that had steered the juggernaut Europe onto a new path.

I dropped into time and space; I was freed from my prison. So many years and lives converged on that point, where those two scratches on the wall met. If this Archduke had not received his power—if Rudolph, the son of Francis Joseph, had not killed himself at Mayerling—if Francis Joseph had been shot dead, at the age of twenty-eight, by that bullet that just missed him at the Battle of Solferino in 1859—1859—if I had not survived out of the children buried at the churchyard of Grahovo—lives upon lives, going back along a line of unknown Serbian peasants, and a line of dukes and princesses starting in a tenth-century castle in the Swiss mountains—Schiller's Delicatessen vanished, the orchards and gardens returned, the Latin Bridge was wooden and narrow once more, the embankments were gone and the horizontal scratch on my wall was the Miljacka between flowery banks, the Mosque and the Turkish faces had gone, now there was only a ferry at that converging point, a Serbian ferryman, wooden houses along the river of shepherds and farmers, not peasants but men growing their own wheat and wine for the far cities of Mostar and Bielgorod, that cross point had existed, then and before, and it had always waited for me.

And for him. For I had not been standing there like the Ludwig Klaus jewel thief in Vienna brandishing a pistol. He himself had conjured me up. Saint-Just: the armed resistance of the people.

71

Then a delirious longing for color and for softness. The rough wall, the moist floor, the rusty chains hurt to the touch and were meant to hurt. But bodies are tenacious and mine still had moments when it tried to overrule my thoughts and this unnatural surrounding, and when I tried to touch my skin through the layer of filthy clothes, to find warmth, to sense. Only once, in those first months, did I open my trousers and put my hands on my prick, in a desperate rubbing, come, damn, come, in an obscene tableau of an old man trying in vain, that dying pope who had young girls put on top of his carcass; I was in this frenzy, looking up at the crossed bars in case a guard was staring, and then again at myself, my sex no part of me but fleshy, solid, stupid, I felt it slipping away and just made it, some drops on my grayish underpants like bleeding from a glass cut; I muttered to the dead, "Forgive me." Oddly, just then a guard came in, unlocked me from the ring and motioned me to come with him. He led me up the steps I knew from the first night and opened a door to a courtyard. It wasn't bigger than a billiard table, enclosed by blind walls. He spoke to me then; he said, "Twenty minutes," and stood at the door.

No way of not looking at him except by circling around, though the chains burned my ankles. Who had built this weird yard and for what purpose? Its flagstones were covered with tiny scraps of paper and with glassy blobs that I could kick loose; frozen spittle or phlegm, I thought. Other men must walk or stand here, and look up. . . . Finally, I dared look up. High on the walls were barred windows and still higher, the sky. A rectangle of white. At the bottom of a shaft, a shaft in this men mine, in the darkest most hidden middle of the sick Empire, I am open, out. There's nothing between my head and, and infinity. I leaned against the wall with my head tilted back, falling to pieces into the sky. Until the guard tapped me on my arm and took me back to the cell.

Romanticism of jails, mystique of jails. Those words spooked in my mind. Somewhere, in some memoir (how many books hadn't been written by imprisoned men) I once read: the romanticism of the nineteenth century, of dark forests and lakes, has now been replaced by the romanticism of jails.

I had not understood. I had thought the writer was thinking of Count of Monte Cristo stuff, secret passages, escapes. You cannot escape from a jail that they do not want you to escape from. Escape stems from compromise. I knew that already then. I knew it through Michael Bakunin, who lived for ten years chained to a Prussian rockface. It doesn't need walls and guards to keep a man. These are to wear him down. It only needs twenty-four pounds of iron on his arms and legs. The mystique of jails was not escape through tunnels or with keys brought by jailers' daughters.

Now I did understand. It was something else. Purity.

Those poets who wandered along the shores of dreamed lakes and wrote about truth and beauty, who had put themselves outside the crass society they despised—at the end of the day they had warm rooms waiting, with roast beef and eiderdowns. I forgave them; they knew no better. But now that no longer held good. In this vile twentieth century the only beauty and truth is in not dirtying yourself with the blood squeezed out of men. Don't share the spoils. The receiver of stolen goods is more despicable than the robber.

A poet now belonged in prison; no true poet could refuse the purity of prison.

Politics are my salvation.

Since childhood I'd had a dream that frightened me. It had its source in those Grahovo evenings when all the people of the village came together to listen to songs and poems, always about our heroes and our broken past. They packed into the room of one peasant or another, and the logs in the fireplace gave the only light, penetrating in beams through the thick smoke made by the wood and the men smoking their pipes. You couldn't distinguish the men and the women clearly in that brown fog, only their eyes, gleaming, reflecting the flames.

In my dream, they always looked at me, and with a kind of reproach, of threat. Now that dream came back without the fear. They and I looked at each other and that was all. And for the first time, my father and mother were there.

That way I got back to my parents. At no interrogation had they ever been mentioned. I pinned my hope on that, that they'd been left alone. I felt longing as everyone must feel, but without pain. I thought perhaps my mother was secretly happy with me. I had avoided thinking about them, as I avoided thinking about my childhood. I stuck to the circle Sarajevo–Belgrade–Sarajevo. Of course, Grahovo lay within that circle. This fortress didn't; it was no part of my real life. Grahovo was those two snow months of brooding. It wasn't being a child or herding sheep.

I shied away from dreams that seemed too private. I was still worried about vanity; I wanted to root out private vanities as fanatically as those hermits on pillars wanted to root out their sins.

I didn't want to be a twentieth-century Kosovo hero any more. I thought I knew now that the twentieth century does not need heroes. Not even folk heroes. It needs community.

72

In prison, the day is twenty hours, the night four. I always woke hours before it got light. Then I lay motionless and felt that all human thought, that all humanity was going through my head. Books signify life to me. Now, even the cold was less hard than their ban on reading and on writing. Because of this bent in me, my thoughts often were too far-flung for my friends' taste. That in turn made me a silent man in their meetings. But when I read or wrote or thought, everything was terribly, painfully clear to me. I mistrusted the simple truths of men who have power. The truth is not simple. Kropotkin and Saint-Just were not simple. All fight and suffering end up in me. Only the politician and the businessman are afraid of the word *but*.

I saw all the good thoughts that people ever had in this world through all time rise in the sky, the air was filled with them, indestructible, going through stone and wood, a blanket of happiness. Or a stream, maybe, clear and warm like the Amazon River, or a spring of water, or a fire—whatever you were most desperate for.

They were that for me. Fire. Water.

I could tell that the winter was nearing its end. At dawn, the cold was less satanic. I couldn't see my breath during the day, and when they took me for another outing in the yard, the ground was slippery, not frozen any more. The sky rectangle was blue, pure blue. Color. And a bird flew overhead before the twenty minutes was up. I thought about it through a spring and a summer. But only a day had gone by.

My towel stuck to my forehead one morning after washing. Terrible pain to pull it off. I discovered that those Sarajevo lesions had started oozing again, months after they had closed. And once while eating I hit the wall with my left elbow just lightly, and the shock was so sudden and sharp that I dropped the tin and fell to the floor. I touched my arm, the bone in the elbow felt softened, I felt it give under my finger with a sickening ache. My fever came back then, for something had gone wrong in my body but I couldn't focus on it.

Only when I was standing naked in the washroom for the monthly change, did I see I had a strange sore on my chest and one on my left arm, in places where I hadn't been wounded before. Pus came out and it looked furry. "I'm growing fungus," I said to myself. I saw the guard stare at it. That evening I was sitting on the floor in a stupor and didn't even notice when my guard came in. He must have got impatient for he pulled me up by my wrist chain. It felt as if he had torn off my arm and I passed out.

I came to, buckled to a stretcher, not in the cell but in a room. I saw a barred window and daylight coming in. I closed my eyes again. It was such a blessing to lie in the light that I wasn't going to make any move that could end it. Much later, a man was touching me. When I opened my eyes, he said "I'm Doctor Levin. I'm Czech, I'm a prisoner, too."

He made a grimace of disgust as he pulled up my undershirt. I then realized that my chains were gone. I heard voices, it got dark, and light again. I was still on the stretcher, now with a blanket over me. Doctor Levin came in with a guard.

"You have to go back to your cell," he said. "There's nothing I can do for you now. Perhaps later."

To the guard he said, "I'd leave off the chains."

The guard shrugged without answering. He turned to the door.

"What is it?" I asked the doctor.

"You got tuberculosis. Of the bones, I think."

I couldn't think what to ask next. Nothing seemed to apply.

"I'll try to get to see you again," he said and shook my hand.

The guard held my arm and rather gently led me back to the cell. He sat me down on my bunk and put the irons back on, but he didn't pull the chain through the ring on the wall; not that day.

I opened my hand when he had gone. Through the muddy air of my cell rose the smell of chocolate. The doctor had put a piece of chocolate in my hand, wrapped in a sheet from a notebook.

I read, "Cabri has died. But Trifko is in good spirits. You have friends, don't give up."

I read and reread that message, while I chewed as slowly as possible on my piece of chocolate.

73

The last houses of Sarajevo are on one side of the road we're walking. A cow pasture faces them, with a farm in the distance picked out by the low sun against the trees. Sophia, silent, keeps turning her face toward me with an almost-secret smile.

A man, waiting near the fountain in Terazije, and a woman who appears out of the evening with hasty steps. He kisses her fleetingly but deep in her neck, I hear them whisper as I pass them.

A girl seen on a balcony, turning around and saying to someone invisible, "Yes, it's going to rain. But the air is soft." You could tell from her voice she was talking to a man, a total intimacy.

Girl. Une femme. Ragazza, a lovely word. Hunger for a feeling never known.

Images of the roundness and the tension of a woman's body and of her skin. Of moving your hand from her shoulder over her breasts, down, over her belly, to that smoothness where her belly and her thighs meet and everything is directed inward. To be in a girl. An unbelievable idea. To kiss that flat softness. To be embraced, by cool nude arms, a sweet mysterious face, as mysterious as her belly, as being in her. Like night, like I don't know what. I would have wanted to know.

No. Damn that niceness and softness and nostalgia. I want to think of fucking. Of a girl's cunt.

I don't know how to. I can't conjure up anything except a major in the Blue Star brothel staring at me over the head of some poor creature, except men, ugly naked men. Two dogs with panting tongues on top of each other.

Sophia saves me. I know closeness with her. Once we embraced, in the river orchard of my memory Sarajevo where they later built a quay and a wall. Leaves and shade glided over her skin.

She is sixteen now. Or perhaps seventeen. Her body rounder, tenser. Her face more serious still.

74

Cold. It was still early spring. Or perhaps the summer of the year 1915, our forbidden year, had already gone. No warmth can penetrate these walls. I have lost track.

My body began caving in. I hated it but I couldn't make it obey. It oozed and I couldn't stop it. I tried to wash the sores. I tried to grind down my talons of nails on the wall, to warm my shoes in the morning by putting the tin with drink in them. I tore edges off the blanket with my teeth and wrapped them around my hands.

They took me to the prison hospital again one day when I had passed out. Another doctor there painted my sores with iodine. I asked him where Doctor Levin was and he said, "He's dead."

Then he looked at the guard, worried that he'd be taken to task for speaking to me, but the guard gave him an odd grin and said, "And a good thing, too. One less of 'em."

The doctor turned red. He seemed to wait for me to answer something to that. It was such a strange turnabout that I couldn't get the nerve together. I looked at the guard without saying a word.

"And as for you," the guard said to me, "Serbia's had it, too."

"What?" I whispered.

"Serbia's been overrun. Gone, kaput. The army is hiding out in Greece or some such place."

I shook my head, and looked at the doctor.

"Yes, that is true," he said slowly. "Austria-Hungary—"

"Austria-Hungary my ass," the guard interrupted. "It's our army, the German army, with the Bulgarians, that defeated them. For you must give it to them, the Serbians were good fighters. The Austrians—they're swindlers, not soldiers."

The doctor put the iodine bottle down and left the room.

The guard laughed. "Fucking Jews," he said. He eyed me and asked, "Don't you agree?"

And then in a kind of stage whisper, "How about splitting some of that gold with me?"

"Well, you fellows all have Russian gold stashed away somewhere, don't you?" he insisted.

"You aren't allowed to talk to me," I murmured.

He heard me. "I'll be damned," he said. "Try to be nice to them. Just goes to show. Hey, your friend is dead, do you know?"

I nodded.

"No, you can't know. It happened yesterday."

After a moment he said, "Yes, Grabez. That's right. Trifko Grabez. Death from natural causes."

When I was back in my cell, my bread of two days was sitting there, on top of the tin with the potatoes of the evening before.

I took a bite of bread and spit it out. It goes hard with my people. And I'm very sick, too sick. They hadn't chained me to the wall. I took my towel, twisted it like a rope and led it through the vertical bar in the window. I knotted the ends together and turned it to get a loop, and there was just enough space to get my head through, standing on the tips of my toes. A terrifying effort. And it was a marvelous relief to stop, to stop it all and to let my legs go.

But the rotten towel broke or maybe the knot gave way. I fell on the floor and lay still with my head against the door. Tears ran down my face, tears, tears.

75

A doctor in a white coat came in, together with a soldier. But there was no room and the soldier posted himself outside the door. He wasn't one of those guards in their stained overalls, but an infantryman in field uniform, with fixed bayonet.

The doctor sat on my bunk and said, "I've come to have a talk with you."

"Doctor Levin thought I got tuberculosis, of the bones."

"Well, no," he said, "I'm not here for that. I'm a psychiatrist. I'm here to work with our shell-shock cases in the open hospital. But I'm also interested in other—other—I've permission to conduct some interviews with you. Are you willing to co-operate? I'm Doctor Pappenheim, lecturer at the University of Vienna. I'm not a spy." This with a heavy smile.

"Other what?"

"I beg your pardon?"

"You're interested in other what?"

"Mental problems," he said.

"Why did you bring a soldier with you?" I asked Pappenheim.

"Tell me first if you will co-operate. I'd love to chat with you, but otherwise I cannot."

"Yes."

"He's here to guard you. I didn't bring him. There are two more. Headquarters in Leitmeritz sent them. They must think you're about to escape."

"I know I can't escape." Then I began to laugh, it sounded to me like an old dog barking.

He must have thought his irony had been too inimical. "One never knows what happens next in war," he announced. "Why did you laugh just now?"

I wasn't going to tell Pappenheim what a weight had been lifted off me.

Their tricks always have the opposite effect. No more suicides. Fuck them. I was going to outlive their Empire. Lecturer from Vienna. Leitmeritz Headquarters knew better. If they thought I was worth three soldiers, three uninvalided infantrymen, with three rifles and three bayonets, in the middle of their war, then I'd stand up to that. Live. Show they are right.

"My mental problems do not fall in your sphere," I said to the doctor. "You should have some interviews with the Emperor."

He pulled out a note pad. "I'd like to make some notes about your childhood, your youth, your motives. Will you let me do that?

To protect themselves? To forestall others? I nodded, though. What were our motives? Revenge and love.

76

A giant green bower.

I am walking with Trifko. Nothing was ever like our walk, and we are trying and trying to recapture it once more. I know

Trifko is dead but it doesn't sadden me; he is there beside me, swishing a branch and hitting the trees with it.

We follow a path through a wood without end, as if it covered the whole world.

I was back in a room, in daylight, and not on a stretcher but on a bunk, and with two blankets.

I couldn't stop myself getting sicker. Two days at the time in the hospital room, and then back to the cell for two months. In the prison hospital my food was the same as in the cell; a slice of bread, turnips or potatoes.

I failed to understand why they shuttled me back and forth. A civilization that starved its prisoners to death and sent them to a doctor as if its own policy were an unknown disease. Like those doctors getting a condemned man back on his feet for his execution; science, as cruel as old rituals and more hypocritical. But the hospital room bathed in a sea of daylight, and with the light came the warmth of the sun. It interrupted the shapeless, cold, gray glue of hour, day, month following and following, and whether they intended it this way or not, that saved me.

Pappenheim made an appearance in the hospital room. It was he who had broken that silence of one, two, ten ? years in which I had spoken three sentences. I wasn't grateful; I was turned inside out by it. Now I was overeager to talk. I must be careful.

He had a table and a chair brought in. On the table he put with great precision a stack of paper, and a new pencil. "If you can sit up," he said, "I want you to write down your ideas on the subject 'social revolution.'"

He helped me to the chair, and then stood by the window, peering out over the frosted glass panes. I wasn't tall enough to see over them. I wondered what that window looked out on.

I sat there quietly and stared at the paper. How beautiful a sheet of white paper is, what a lovely invitation. If I could only steal a piece and smuggle it back to my cell with the pencil.

Pappenheim was watching me.

"It's been too long," I said. "My thoughts are muddled. . . .

If, if I could have something to read, just a day or two, I could pull myself together, and do what you want."

He didn't bite. "Just do the best you can."

I thought I'd write down some general ideas, for I didn't want him to give up on me.

I wrote, "We debated revolution, and nearly all of us agreed it was possible. But according to our convictions, there must previously be created in Europe, between peoples, a political—"

I had thought I was pretending when I said I couldn't write anything and needed some books to read first. But I hadn't been pretending. I couldn't go on.

"A political organization," I wrote. "Danilo—"

I broke off.

"Who is Danilo?" he asked. He was reading over my shoulder.

"Danilo was Danilo Ilic. He was hanged. I can't go on. I'm too nervous."

That was his last visit. He took all the paper with him, too, and the pencil.

He left me sitting at the empty table, the soldier, who was now always there, on guard at the door. A strange scene. But it was good to sit at a table in the light of day. I fell into a dreamless sleep with my head on my arm.

Later, the real doctor, again another one, woke me. He was old and seemed friendly. He bandaged my arm and chest, and his manner made me aware that he wasn't supposed to do that for me.

He turned his back to the soldier and said almost soundlessly, "You must know that I am under orders not to talk to you."

I nodded.

"I want to ask permission from Leitmeritz to amputate your lower left arm. Would that scare you?"

I shook my head.

"The request will have to go to Vienna. That's how they are. Still. It will help slow the disease. And you will have less pain afterward."

When they took me back to the cell, they put irons on my feet only, with the chain through the ring. From then on, my left arm was bandaged and my right arm was free.

I decided to start my calendar on the wall again, with a piece of stone out of the floor, which was cracked where the bunk was screwed in.

I made a guess that it was the first of October of the year 1916. I made columns for the weeks and months from then on.

It was hard work. I had to stop and sit down on the floor. It is terrible when they've made your body your own enemy. A stain was spreading on the bandage. Calm down. That's the bad stuff draining off.

1916. Two years gone. No, it cannot be, it is spring. It could be, could it be, the spring of 1917? I did not know any more. I think that only at that moment was it brought home to me, that I was left alone in that stone mountain with the obscene name Theresienstadt, a town on another planet, unknown and unseen by anyone I had ever loved. Danilo, Cabri, Trifko were dead. Now the Emperor was waiting for me to die, to declare it all over and forever forgotten.

"What year is it?" I screamed. And banged the chains on the floor. I had never done a thing like that. The guard would come and shut me up, give me a bash on the head. But when I stopped and listened, there were only the soft steps of the soldier in the corridor, going back and forth without interruption. No, no steps. Three feet of wall. I was being funny, Pappenheim, no need to make a note. But I knew those steps were there, which is like hearing them.

77

No one talked to me for a very long period after that old doctor. He was gentle. But I got a hold on myself. For even within my cell, I knew there was a turnabout. You cannot hide it from me. There is a change in the affairs of the Empire. Outside it, suspended like a hanged man, I know.

They hadn't counted on that. They had forgotten we are southerners, not scientific Germans. Intuitions come to our aid. Or perhaps it was scientific observation. A near-invisible change in the face of the guard who unlocks my chain and puts the cup on the floor. There is so little light but he comes so close to me. I see the gray stubble on his gray skin, the vacant eyes that do not see me. He stinks too. He has to, not to mind me. Perhaps the coming doom of his Empire can be read in those lines going down from his nose. Perhaps he moves an inch per second slower. Or faster.

I can hold out now. Until a Serbian will unlock my door, and kiss me. Brother, give me your brotherhand. I thought of the young man in Belgrade run over by an automobile, death for no reason.

I know my friends are dying, bullets and dynamite and metal splinters killing them. I wish—I want to be with them. I don't want to freeze and be patched up and freeze, I don't want to be patched up any more in the thick nauseating silence behind these German stones, I want to freeze in our blessed mountains and to be patched up or die with others, not by myself, not in silence, but in shattering noise, I want to die with voices and explosions all around me.

But I am the last one of us here; I must, I must—what. Push myself through, make it. For some reason. Which one. Well, if you don't, I tell myself, it's all been such a sad mess. That's the best I can do now as far as reasons are concerned. I finish my bread, I eat a potato, I dream, I eat my bread, I exist.

78

Now it had become very dark and cold. Perhaps winter again. They took me back to the old doctor.

He had permission to operate. "We'll have you washed and shaved first," he said. For I had a beard that always itched.

I sat in a chair in the hospital room, and a prisoner appeared with a box and a basin of warm water. He muttered a greeting to the soldier, I think it was in Polish, and he didn't say anything to me. I had seen him before; he had come to the washroom to cut off my hair. After he'd cut the beard and soaped my face, he brought out a strop for his razor, and he looked around for a place to put down the wet brush. He gave it to me to hold, with a terrible grimace and a twist of his hand.

I found that the handle of the brush was loose and came out. A folded strip of paper was hidden in it.

When he was done shaving, he held a little mirror up for me. I was surprised to see my own face, very thin with dark hollow eyes. I didn't look older, more like a solemn child of twelve. It was a nice feeling to stroke my chin.

They let me sit there for a long time, alone with the soldier. I took hasty looks at the slip of paper. The writing was small and I had to take a word at a time.

"Greetings. I am a Serb officer. In prison here but for a short sentence. Rumania is in the war on our side. America is in the war on our side. The Austrian front lines are chaos, desertion. Poison gas is now used as a weapon."

A heavy exclamation mark, and an arrow.

I turned the paper, eyed the soldier, and looked again.

"Revolution in Russia!!! The Czar has abdicated. We will win. This Empire will go next. God bless Young Bosnia."

I rolled the slip into a little ball to swallow it, but I couldn't. I had to read those words again, I had to keep those words. When the doctor came back in, I still clutched the paper in my hand.

Then he started faster than I had expected. He didn't make a big production of an amputation; at the front he must do twenty a day. He sprinkled ether on a piece of gauze and put it over my face, and that was that.

I was traveling in a carriage or an automobile, it wasn't clear. I have never been in an automobile, but there seemed to be no horses. We went at great speed along a road, without a jolt, and in and out of tunnels through the mountainside. Then we rolled down into the Sarajevo plain. I don't remember who "we" were, but at one point I looked around and saw my father and mother sitting behind me, very pleased, and younger and less bent than I had ever seen them.

We entered a town without lessening speed. To my bewilderment, it wasn't Sarajevo but a place I had never seen. It was a large town. Large buildings, covered with black flags, flew by and people on each side of the street. No one looked at us. I was now sitting next to a coachman. He pointed with his whip at the people, and where he pointed there'd be an outburst of shouts. I thought they were inimical, and tried to take the whip out of his hand. But he struck my hand aside. And now I realized that the shouting wasn't angry. They were cheering, though they stared beyond us. I saw that the flags hanging down from the houses weren't black either, but white; it was the play of light and shadow that had made them seem black first. If you looked at the ripples, you could see exactly how the sun struck them and showed the black to be really white. But we've won, I thought, white flags. And of course it was Sarajevo. I wondered how I could not have recognized it before. I was so relieved that I stood up in the box and waved. A child in a sailor's suit, a child in a sailor's suit—I waited for it to wave back—"Watch it!" the coachman shouted and I saw we were making straight for a wall across the road. I looked back, my parents were still sitting there, but they were dead, the skin was peeling off their skulls. Then I got very scared. The coachman pulled the reins so hard that I fell, but he didn't pull hard enough, we hit the wall and went through it, I found myself in a small courtyard, no pain, but I was bleeding streams of the gluey white pus, I was in Theresienstadt, in the fortress, in the chair, and I came to.

The doctor was looking at me. He asked if I felt all right.

I turned my head. My left arm ended at the elbow in a thick round bandage. I had to throw up, from the ether, or maybe because it was a big shock after all, and hurt badly.

He wiped my face. "You can sit here and rest a bit," he said. "Do you want a glass of water?"

I startled myself by answering, "Could I have a glass of milk?"

He was surprised, too. "Milk. . . !" he said. "Even we don't see much milk. The Empire isn't doing so well. If they knew I had used all that ether and bandages on you, they'd lock me up in the next cell." And then, "I found a ball of paper in your right hand."

I looked at the door. No soldier. "He's gone to the canteen or maybe to see his girl friend," the doctor announced. "I told him there was no need to stand guard over an unconscious boy. You must be very pleased with your news."

I didn't know if it was a challenge. "Oh, yes," I tried to shout.

He walked to the window and back. "Well, I'm a Ukrainian by birth. And more to the point, I am an old man. I confess," he said very softly, I could hardly hear him, "that it's a good thing if the Austrian and German Empires lose this war. It would certainly be a terrible thing if they won it. They would be intolerable. The furor teutonicus. But I'm too old-fashioned to rejoice at the idea of those Bolsheviks and Mensjeviks getting to power in Russia. I'm scared of that kind of New World. And they say that's what will happen."

I just smiled at him. It was staggering to hear someone calmly discuss revolution in Europe as a reality. I would forget my arm. The taste of ether.

I tried to answer. He gave me some water to drink, and added, "Wouldn't it have been better if Russia had remained a strong Czarist Empire, fighting the German Empire? I want you to know that I've never believed you and your friends were criminals. I thought you were idealists."

I said, "You've been kinder, doctor, than— Don't worry. All will be well, at last."

"I hope you're right."

"This is what we've hoped for. If the war—" I couldn't organize my words and I got tears of frustration in my eyes.

He said to calm down, he was listening.

"If the war comes out with, with empires defeating empires, nothing much— But now—"

That's not what I wanted to say.

He looked away from me, out of the window, which helped. I knew now what I had to tell him. "You said you are too old, about Russia I mean. You're wrong. Revolution is about, is to get back to an old, forgotten, common, natural, way of life. It is Communism that is old-fashioned."

I don't think I explained myself properly. I drank water.

"That New World you're scared of is here. It is our world. It's what we have now. Mad greed, money. The iron world."

He was still at the window. "Yes, perhaps," he answered. "Perhaps you're right."

"Doctor," I asked, "what's outside that window?"

He turned in surprise, and then he very calmly and effortlessly took me in his arms and lifted me up. I saw a tree, I didn't know what kind, but it was a beautiful tree, in leaf. Soft green shapes, not man made. Leaves.

79

The last real thing I did in my cell was to start writing a poem on the wall. In case I failed to make it, they'd find—

> Our ghosts will travel to Vienna
> will wander through the palaces,
> ask for reckoning from kings

I don't know if I got much further, I don't remember. After that, all I could do was sit quietly on the floor. I didn't scratch down the days on the wall, no point in it. My blanket was over me, I lived as in a tent; no guard interfered with that any more. As when we played Indians or Bedouins as children. I had read in a book long ago about a Red Indian who had tried to stop a white man's train with his lasso. He had succeeded in lassoing the engine but of course only killed himself. No one even saw it happen, when the train pulled in, they only found the rope and his arms, still clutching it. I cried over that as a child. I tried not to start crying again. Why do people roam so murderously all over the world? To be rich? Would my people do the same one day?

No.

No. Not good works, not philanthropic ladies and missionary priests. Social revolution between quotes, just wait, Lecturer Pappenheim, wait and read our words on "social revolution."

You won't be able to fit them in the curriculum of Vienna University.

Then again gusts of doubt, sudden cold fears, blew through my tent. Was it good? Wasn't the most miserable Orthodox peasant happier than the happiest man without misery and without God? Wasn't the fear of death the greatest load on earth? But as that fear is there anyway. And turns men into choking greedy— Greed flays slaves alive, burns down our farms, kills, kills. I kill a million Chinese for a crown each, that was the ethical problem of our high school professor. The total incapacity of any man to feel what another man feels— except a revolutionary, who tries to. The little smiles on the faces of the soldiers who hang their fellow men and women, who perforate a peasant's skin with their bayonet, let it enter his unresisting bowels, eight inches regulation depth, one turn, kick it out. The same men who curse when they burn a finger on a match. I want to be away from this earth, I no longer have the strength to understand my fellow beings. They look like me, but they are as unlike me as if they were lizards or cats. More so. Lizards don't torture. Cats are innocent. I am innocent. Their Jesus, your Jesus didn't have himself crucified to take our sins away, but because he could no longer understand them.

What do life and death mean? Why are we cursed with consciousness? Isn't that by itself hell, just that, without flames or sulphur, what pain could be greater? What difference does it make then, sick or healthy, young or old, one or two arms, hungry or fed? What difference in eternity between the Emperor eighty-five years old in his palace and a baby killed at birth? Why try to register justice, emotions, love, pleasure, during our lives when all is obliterated forever? Who'd write a book on paper that will be burned when he's finished?

But I would have liked to live some other lives. I would have liked to be a seaman too, on a small ship bound for Brazil or Mexico. To be a wise man in the Himalaya Mountains. A bar owner in a port where the whistles of steamships would wake me in the morning, and the sun over the water. To be Sophia.

To be a child in Russia, in their new life, born there just now, never to have known the old.

What have I done with my one and only life?

Within what I understand of the mystery, my life makes sense to me. The fields of the earth are crisscrossed by bones. What's there to say? We are meant to die at the end of our days, in peace; meant by whom? Well, simply by our bodies, if nothing else. Aren't our bodies meant for seventy years or eighty years, just like a tree is meant for two hundred years and a butterfly for a day? I think I've lived just at the dawn of my species, man. That is lucky.

I sit on the floor in my blanket tent and I retell my story in my mind.

80

I am telling my story in my mind. It's crucial for me not to fall into any traps of turning for myself what happened into a personal drama. If I did, I would be alone. And I am not.

When the last light in the corridor is about to go, when I can just distinguish the cross of the two bars in the little half-circle window of my cell door against the grayness behind it, the guard comes and unlocks my chain from its ring in the stone. Then I can get back to my bunk and lie down for the night. He never says a word to me. While the door is open, I can hear the step of the soldier on duty in the passage.

I put the chain under the blanket with me. I used to keep it outside my cover, but I discovered it drained off my body's warmth that way. So now I sleep embracing my chain with my arm. The smell of the rust and iron is overwhelming. I have never gotten used to it. It makes me retch every morning before the tin of barley coffee and the bread help me right myself. Before the guard hands me these, he fixes my chain back in the ring. I can stand then, or sit on the floor under my blanket.

Time, hesitantly, starts to move through my head.

Then there was nothing left to do but to wait.

Great peace descended on me and enveloped me.

It was warm. I could do without my blanket now.

People entered my cell, everyone I knew, and also strangers. Many of them had died. They came and went, mostly they were gentle. I wasn't afraid of any of them. I was never afraid any more. None of them spoke, but then everything had been said. Just to see Cabri, and my father, and—

I lay on my bunk in my cell. There was daylight seeping in: they hadn't made me get up. I must be doing badly. But I knew I'd live.

I saw gleaming boots around me. Officers were standing there.

"This is Princip, General," someone said.

And another voice said, "Prisoner Princip, I am inspecting this prison. Do you have any complaints to make?"

I began to laugh, but they didn't hear me, for there was no reaction.

Then the General said, "Princip, I would like to use this occasion to ask you if you have repented your deed?"

I saw his face quite clearly now.

"It is for you to repent, General," I think I answered, "for your Empire is doomed. And so is the state of being a General."

But when I heard the door lock squeak, I tried to call them back. I should have spoken with more love.

For I want to love everyone. People aren't wicked; they are just sad, and pathetic.

They must be lifted up like small children and have their tears dried.

I love everyone. I forgive Francis Ferdinand of Austria-Este.

Gavre died on the 28th of April, 1918. He almost made it. Only six more months, and the vast Empire that had used his deed to go to war had broken up because of that war.

He died at half past six in the evening. The light had vanished from the cells, but the sun was still a hand's width over the horizon of Theresienstadt and its last rays lit up the outer guard room where the soldiers on night duty sat around. One of these was a local young man, a Czech called Frantisek.

It isn't possible to understand, to take the measure, of the loneliness in which Gavre survived those years and in which he died. The very act of doing so would seem to diminish that loneliness.

For Gavre didn't tell his story to any living being. There was no echo to these words in his mind—not until after his mind had gone. They are heard only after his death, from beyond that grave he now shares with his three friends in a Sarajevo field. They are heard by us now living, under more overbearing satraps, in more subtle and more wicked Empires.

That Czech soldier who was on guard duty in the night of April 28, 1918, told me:

At eleven that evening, the duty lieutenant called me and three others to his office. We saw a large wooden box, the kind we ship rifles in. He told us to take it in a horse van to the Roman Catholic cemetery. We'd find a hole there, dug in the footpath to the entrance gate. We had to put the box in that hole, fill it up, and smooth over the path. And he talked about the full weight of Austrian military discipline that would fall on our heads if we ever afterward discussed it.

We looked at one another. We knew already that the rifle box was now the coffin of Gavrilo Princip who had died a few hours before, just as we came on. But we didn't comment and carried the box into the yard where the vans were parked.

By the time we had come to the cemetery, it had started to rain again, as it did every day in that cursed spring of 1918. It was pitch-dark and we had only one lantern. We stumbled around in the mud for half an hour before we found the hole, half hidden in a curve of the lane by a hedge. We couldn't get the van all the way up there and carried the box ourselves. It was not heavy at all. Then we filled in the hole and smoothed the wet sand and the pebbles over it till it was invisible. But as we rode back to the fortress, I memorized that place, the curve, the hedge, and the gate, and when we went off duty, I sketched it on the back page of my Soldier's Paybook. No one would understand those scribbles.

Our Empire collapsed and accepted an armistice on the third of November 1918. It was a Sunday. I was at the front of Treviso then, in a rear echelon, living in a mud shelter, marking time like a million other men afraid to be shot for desertion if we climbed out and walked home one day too soon. But an hour after they blew the cease-fire there wasn't a man left there. I couldn't get on a van or on a train and walked most of the way home. On the twenty-fifth of November I was back in Theresienstadt.

The town looked terrible. Mud a foot deep, garbage strewn everywhere, no street lights, no gas, no electricity. In the shop windows you saw empty boxes and the stores were bare. Gray, raggy women and children stood in line in the damn rain for the bread ration of two ounces of baked swill. But the mood of our town was fine! The reason was, the Germans and the Austrians were getting out. Theresienstadt was going to be Teresin. On the fortress flew a new red, blue, and white flag, the flag of Czechoslovakia.

I'd have liked to go to my old guard room, get the keys, and go open the cell of Princip. That would have been a fine thing on a day like this.

It was too late.

But I knew where he was buried, I and no one else in the world. I stayed only an hour with my family, and then I went to the cemetery. It was mid-afternoon but it was almost as dark as on that April night. I had the page from my paybook.

The gate was there, the turnings, and the hedge, nothing was changed. I figured it all out till I knew I stood on the precise spot. Then I drew a circle in the earth with a branch, as deep as I could, and kneeled and said a prayer for him. I planted the branch in the ground.

When I got back in town, I saw a booth where two women were selling the new Czechoslovakian flags. I guess it was about the only thing freely for sale at that time in Teresin-Theresien-stadt. They weren't very good flags, but they weren't paper. That was a feat, I don't know where they got the cloth.

I stood and looked at them for a while. They weren't Serbian flags of course. The pattern was different. But the colors were the same red, blue, white.

I bought one and took it home. They thought I was crazy, but I waited for my sister to cut it up and sew it together again. I didn't even take my boots off.

Then, in the last light of day, with a bit of red sun through those rain clouds, I walked back on one more trip to the cemetery. My branch had already toppled over and I threw it away. I had brought a rope and a stick from my father's tool box, and I planted over Princip's body the flag of Serbia.